DIANA: A DIARY IN THE SECOND PERSON

T0126271

DIANA

A DIARY IN THE SECOND PERSON

Russell Smith

BIBLIOASIS

FIRST EDITION

Library and Archives Canada Cataloguing in Publication

Smith, Russell, 1963-
Diana : a diary in the second person / Russell Smith.

First ed. published 2003, written by the author
under his pen name, Diane Savage.

ISBN 13: 978-1-897231-39-5
ISBN 10: 1-897231-39-3

I. Title.
PS8587.M58397D52 2008   C813'.54   C2007-907434-0

PRINTED AND BOUND AT THOMSON-SHORE, DEXTER, MI

INTRODUCTION

This book was first published by Gutter Press, Toronto, in 2003, under the pseudonym Diane Savage. The press had recently undergone a change of ownership, and the new publisher was not quite as enthusiastic about literature as my original editor had been. He saved money on binding by using some sort of temporary procedure; the book fell apart on opening. So did the press itself, in fact: it ceased to exist shortly after my book came out. *Diana* had never been well distributed across the country, I suspect because the distributor was owed money.

There was a launch party in Toronto, at a bar called Lava Lounge. It was a quiet affair, about 50 people, even though we had sent invitations to all my friends. No one outside the literary business guessed that the book was written by me, even though I had been talking about writing pornography for the previous year. We had hired an actress to read an excerpt from it, and I paid her from my pocket.

Of course, some of the literary media already knew the author's identity. Toronto is a small place, and everyone knows or is indeed married to everyone. I remember seeing Noah Richler, then book critic for the *National Post*, at the party, and warmly shaking his hand and asking him if he would like a beer. He seemed friendly enough. I left him to go and chat up a tall and very pretty woman who turned out to have a charming Polish accent. She later said that I seemed obnoxious and full of myself. I must have been in a good mood.

The next day, the *National Post* appeared, containing an article about this book, and revealing its author. It was the most vitriolic denunciation of my work, and of me generally, that I had ever read. (At least it was until a couple of years later, when the next attack in the *National Post* came, this time denouncing me for having written a book on men's fashion, which the author of that piece also apparently deemed pornographic.)

It was nasty, personal, derisive and utterly dismissive – not just of this book, but of the weekly column that I wrote in the *Globe and Mail*, and basically of the way I lived my life. It was written by Noah Richler.

Richler was disgusted by this book. I think that he was disgusted by pornography generally, by the idea of pornography. Basically, he was embarrassed.

I was, let's say, surprised. Had I not seen Noah at the launch party? Had he not enjoyed the free beer and the attendant tall Polish girls? I seemed to recall him listening to the reading at least. And, wait a minute – when did he have time to write the article? Did he write it all late at night and submit it for the latest possible deadline, like a reporter covering an election or a prize fight? That kind of breathless, stop-the-presses antici-pation of a book review seemed doubtful, particularly in the not-very-literary *National Post*. He must have written at least most of it before the party. In other words, he came to the party, smiling and shaking my hand, knowing that he was about to demolish me the very next day, and in the most *ad hominem* manner.

I am still to this day stupefied by the balls that it took to do this. I don't know if it was naive or malicious.

At any rate, that was how long my anonymity lasted: one night. About 12 hours. The game was up.

What was the game? Why had I tried to pass myself off as a woman? (And as a rather mousey, conservative woman, at that: the original bio-graphical note for Diane Savage said that she was a married schoolteacher who lived in the small town of Cobourg with her three children.)

First, because I wanted women to read it, and I did not want them prejudiced. For they would be: there is a tendency to sneer at all erotic writing, particularly in this country, and that tendency is exaggerated when the writing is by a male. My narrative is from a woman's point of view (for reasons I will get to in a minute), and I could see it being quickly dismissed as inauthentic. I knew that whatever fantasies I dra-matized in the book, even those that I had heard women describing (and in fact they are all, every one, fantasies which I had heard women describing), they would be dismissed as male. I knew that since my pro-tagonist was a submissive, this explanation would be even more popular. (Of course a man would want a woman to be submissive, right, and isn't that sexist bullshit?)

Why did I want women to read it? First, because women are the market you want for any work of fiction: they are pretty much the only readers of fiction left, and particularly of erotic fiction, of which they are, statistically, the only readers. There wouldn't be much point in publishing a work of pornography that women wouldn't read. There was no other market.

But secondly, and more deeply, the whole project came out of attempts at seduction: mine, of specific women.

I've never been much of a stud. I get nervous trying to pick women up, and even more nervous when I get them home. I can't offer any particular expertise on sexual technique. It took me until well into my thirties to discover what my particular sexual talent was. It was (unsurprisingly, I suppose) talking.

I happened on it by accident. I kept pressing a girlfriend to tell me her darkest fantasies, the ones she would be embarrassed and ashamed of. I wanted to know for the same reason one watches pornography on film: it turned me on. So she did. And it did. So I remembered what she told me. And the next time we were together in darkness, I started murmuring in her ear, telling a similar story.

This turned out to be effective. It turned out to be the most erotic thing I could do with my body. And the darker my stories grew – the more they involved restraint and strangers – the more effective they appeared to be. My words appeared to hasten orgasm, and the dirtier the words, the more violent the orgasm.

So I pressed my partner, and all my subsequent partners, to tell me the fantasies that I could embellish into detailed stories, which I would then use, for entirely selfish purposes, the next time we were in bed, or driving on a large highway or waiting for a lecture to start. I have stolen all of these whispered admissions and extrapolated them into this book. (The use of the second person reflects this genesis: these tales began as murmured instructions, given to a specific listener, to put herself into this fantasy. They are stage directions.)

More than one male writer has admitted that his primary motivation in writing fiction was to impress women. I'm sure that race car drivers and accountants would, if they were honest, admit to similar desires behind their drive for success. These things aren't conscious, but I would guess that even my non-pornographic fiction was driven in large part by the desire to be noticed and admired by girls.

But then the experience of writing fiction, even non-pornographic fiction, has always been erotic for me. There is something about immersing oneself in a fantastic environment, in imagining its smells and its textures, which is unbearably sensual: those colours are heightened, amped up, the way they are in dreams.

And, of course, becoming a woman has to be a part of the fictive enterprise. To create female characters you must inhabit them. It's something I had already done in a number of stories. (And after writing this book, I went on to write a longer novel, called *Muriella Pent*, which revolved around a woman, and her sex life in particular; it was the longest stretch I had spent inside a woman's body and it came much easier, I think, after writing *Diana*.)

Did I feel bad about practising a deception on my readers, by claiming to be a woman? Yes, I did, which is why I am relieved to be abandoning the fraud here.

Why did that imagined woman have to be submissive? Because most of the fantasies I heard from female friends involved some degree of passivity, and many even involved coercion. This may be simply because of the kind of woman I am drawn to, of course; they may not be representative of womankind. But they are the stories and images I found to be most effective.

I have my theories as to why. It's easier to lose yourself in a guilt-free sexual fantasy, particularly one which is mildly rough or dangerous, if you picture yourself as not responsible for it: you *couldn't help* being savaged by that massive cock, being watched by that strange amazon, being caressed by that anonymous group – you were tied up, it was forced on you!

Being submissive absolves one of guilt for one's own depravity.

And of course Diana is not entirely submissive: she is pretty domineering with Jones, for example. She takes her own risks. But this is the complicated deceit of submission and dominance: they reflect each other, variations on the same desire for power. Submissives are narcissists: they want to be the centre of attention. Their power is the power to create desire. Someone else is in charge of making the tough decisions on how to get them off – which is another way of being cared for, indulged, pleasured. Diana controls as much as she is controlled, for submission and dominance are the inseparable faces of the same pleasure, a coin that is always spinning.

In a practical sense, this book was an exercise: an exercise in writing as a woman, and an exercise in writing unexpurgated sex. I had noticed in my other fiction that I was too shy in this regard: I tended to abandon sex scenes as they began, panning to the window as the movies do, then cutting to the lovers waking the next morning (or, as was more likely in my somewhat dyspeptic fictitious world, rolling away from each other in disgust). I was puzzled by my own squeamishness in this regard: I'm a horny guy, a guy who gets turned on just by describing a woman's dress in type; what was I afraid of?

I suppose I was succumbing to general pressure, from what I imagined my readers' own embarrassments to be. I was afraid of embarrassing; more importantly, I was afraid of amusing. I had heard of the annual "Bad Sex Award" that the Brits give out for overly florid passages; I knew that our snickering literary media were likely to isolate and quote sex scenes from recent novels as inherently funny – funny simply for existing.

And most sex scenes are embarrassing, when you isolate them. The English language is not suited to graphic descriptions of passionate acts. Writing a whole book of pornography, I was constantly stymied by a paucity of vocabulary: there are only so many words for body parts, and for the actions they perform (for in fact, there are only so many actions), and constant use of them becomes repetitious. And really, none of these words is satisfactory: if you use the correct, everyday word for a body part – penis or vagina, say – you risk sounding cold and clinical, like a medical textbook or a how-to guide. Slang words, on the other hand, tend to be either ugly or humorous. Cock and pussy are harsh and, well, childish, and from a register of language that I suppose you'd have to call proletarian; that register does not suit every scene and every character.

The alternatives, the poetic metaphors, are merely euphemistic – and it's these euphemisms that create the most fun in those Bad Sex Writing competitions: it's all the members and manhoods and Core Of Her Beings that embarrass. It's in trying to make the everyday language less clinical that writers of romance end up writing purple: it's not in naming sex acts, actually, but in *avoiding* that naming, and in spending as much time as possible on the abstract – the spiritual, the emotional sides of sex which are so much more difficult to capture than the stage directions –

that bad sex writers manage to take the physically raw and make it silly and fuzzy.

But it was silly of me, I thought – silly of all of us – to avoid describing that area of conflict and pleasure which is so central to our daily lives, our relationships, our self-confidence, our whole sense of self, simply because it was hard to do. That would be like avoiding writing about food in novels because it's hard to describe flavours: we would have to forgo all the social rituals of eating, all the tensions of the dinner table, all the cultural implications of menus.

I wish there were more sex in books, actually: not more souls melding together in bliss or dancing together like dolphins in heaven or wherever they dance, but sex acts. I want to know exactly what people do, how long they take, whether they both like it, whether they giggle, whether they both get off and how they feel about it afterwards – and I want to know all the awkwardnesses and embarrassments that result. Sex is as complicated and fraught as any human interaction: it seems arbitrary to cut out such a crucial battleground from our stories.

So I decided to wipe out my nervousness about such descriptions, by doing an entire book of them. It worked: there was much more graphic sex in my next (legitimate) novel. In the future I hope and in fact predict that the line between the genres will continue to erode, not just in my fiction but in all fiction: literature will become more pornographic, and pornography will grow more literary. I think this has already begun.

As for the language, in the end I opted to err on the side of the clinical: like a good modernist who grew up on Hemingway and Waugh, I have always tended towards an external gaze in my narration; I don't mind if a scene unfolds more like a movie than an interior monologue. Stage directions again: this is what you are going to do.

Finally, let me address why I use the word pornography and not erotica. I loathe the word erotica: it is cowardly. Erotica is pornography for people who don't want to admit that they like pornography: no coherent philosophical distinction has ever been made between the two. I want to reclaim pornography, say that I like it and that there is nothing wrong with liking it. Pornography is sometimes dismissed as merely practical, as something whose sole purpose is physical arousal. As if there were anything ignoble about such a useful and, to my mind, beautiful goal. And as if so-called "erotica" didn't have exactly the same aim.

10

It's that simple, dear reader: this book is pornography. Its purpose is to titillate. It exists solely to arouse you. It is telling you to position yourself at a window where you can be seen, unbutton your jeans and slip a hand inside the waistband. Now await further instructions.

I

Things aren't going terribly well. It doesn't seem as if your film will ever be produced. You are already fighting with your partners in the company with no name. They have found new boyfriends and are already speaking of engagements and invitations, whereas you have just broken up with lovely, talented, sadly dull Raoul and moved out of the apartment cluttered with instruments and are living alone in a pure white room.

You didn't get the QTV story producer job. You have not worked on your screenplay for some weeks. You must admit that you are stuck.

Really, it is time to face the fact that all you are doing right now is working in a restaurant, the Stoic Grill at that, a sad restaurant which you hate.

You don't want to get mixed up in something as intense as the Raoul thing for a while, moving in with someone before you are really sure, so you are careful about sleeping with your friends, or anyone at the restaurant.

Not that you don't want to. You are aware of men's and women's bodies around you all the time, and you know they are aware of yours. You feel naked all the time. You cast hungry eyes over Jerry the bartender, grateful that he's married so you know you won't do anything stupid with' him (sexy forearms, and pleasant enough, but dumb). You are even noticing the slim thighs of your gay friend Sebastian. (He's getting laid too, and talks about it incessantly. You are happy for him, really.)

You know you are radiating something like a smell these days; you feel taut as you walk down the street and feel men's eyes on you. You can't help walking with a certain serpentine deliberation. You can't help wearing miniskirts to work, or your long stretch velvet dress with the high slit, the dress that clings, that exposes your white shoulders and caresses your breasts into sharp little bumps at the tips.

You have taken to long baths in oil every night, to wearing thong-back panties that tickle you between the buttocks, that grip your sex like a gloved finger, making you always aware – even as you lift trays, pour wine, step on the streetcar – conscious of the lips there, opening and closing.

But nothing happens. You are reading too many romantic novels. You are bored.

You begin reading the personal ads in the free weekly paper that's always lying around the restaurant. You fantasize about what "light dominance" means, or who an "open-minded couple" might be. One ad in particular interests you a little – it seems so straightforward and above board. Models required for nude erotic art photography, $20/hr. No experience necessary; all body types welcome. Photos not for exhibition.

You wonder how erotic "erotic" means. You wonder what the artist does with these photographs if he doesn't exhibit them. You don't even know if it's a he. Although it probably is. Briefly, you picture yourself in a bright warehouse room, an artist's studio, with wind billowing out gauze curtains, standing in a square of sunlight, naked. Or nearly naked: in something white and airy. The sun is on you; points of sweat shine on your chest. Slowly, you are peeling off layers. In the shadows, someone's eyes are on you.

Then you picture a fat old man, some bearded loser with laboured breath, fiddling excitedly with his camera. You forget about it. You go to work.

But late at night, after work, when you have taken your hot, oily bath with your glass of wine, you find yourself looking at your body as if through the appraising eyes of a stranger. It looks so soft and lush; the tuft of hair between your legs so thick and furry.

All week you think about being naked for a stranger, about being admired for your dimpled body. You wonder if other models would be in the room with you as you posed. Or would there be assistants? All pretending to be nonchalant? The thought excites you. You admire your breasts in the mirror when you are alone, stripping slowly for yourself. You like slowly pulling down your panties so the black bush timidly appears. You lie on your front on your bed, imagining a camera at the foot of the bed, and slowly spread you legs. You can't see yourself from behind, but you know that the lips of your sex would be visible. You arch your back so your buttocks rise, so that your crack opens and your sex and asshole are both naked, on display. Your heart beats to think of it. Your groin is swelling and tingling and you know it is making you wet.

The next day you call the number in the ad. You are not surprised to hear a man's voice on the phone, but you are surprised to hear that it is a

14

young voice, young and warm and friendly. But he is businesslike. His name is Patrice; his voice carries a memory of a French accent. He shoots in his studio, which is also where he lives. But it is, he assures you, a large space. He meets all prospective models for an hour, for which of course they are paid, to shoot a few photographs and decide whether he wants to shoot more. He is apologetic that he cannot pay for the models' travelling time as well, as the city is so large, but he is not making any money from these photographs. Of course, should he decide to shoot you, he will book you for three or four hours at a stretch so you earn enough money to make a trip worthwhile.

He seems very thoughtful.

You ask him what to wear, and he says, oh, whatever you feel good in. Whatever makes you feel sexy. And of course, he adds nonchalantly, sexy underwear.

Of course, you say, with a giggle. Your breath catches.

After hesitating a moment, you ask him if he has had much response from his ad. Not much, he says, not enough. A little. You want to ask him how many women have stripped for him, but you do not want to betray any competitive spirit. You know it is not helpful to wonder if you are more beautiful than they are.

You set a time, and he gives you an address in the west end of town, the old industrial district, a zone of train lines and warehouses.

The day, when it comes, is one of the first truly warm days of spring. The trees have just sprouted with the luminous light green which they will only keep for a week, a naive, new green. It rains in the morning, and the sun shines hot in the afternoon on the damp streets. Lawns squelch.

You spend a long time considering your outfit. You settle on a light summer dress, a sundress, loose and translucent, and bare legs. White underwear, like a girl's.

On the way there you are whistled at twice, and a young man in a suit, reading a newspaper, smiles at you at the bus stop. You smile back, frightening him. He hides in his newspaper. You make sure your skirt swings as you step on the bus ahead of him.

The address leads you to a renovated building on a sidestreet, one which you have often passed and noticed, often wondered about, in fact. It was once a factory or warehouse, now obviously artists' studios, but expensive ones, with skylights visible through vast windows. Some of the apartments seem to be open spaces two stories high. Foliage dribbles over the wooden enclosures on the roof, indicating gardens. You can imagine what knowing cocktail parties take place up there, what neurotic barbecues. You are surprised you don't know anybody who lives in this building, as these are the kind of people you tend to know.

He opens the door to his space, smiling. He is a little older than you, maybe early thirties. He has straight blonde hair, swept back. It is an expensive haircut. He wears faded jeans and a bright white T-shirt. The T-shirt is tight enough to reveal a sculpted torso.

He shakes your hand, and you step into one of the two-storey spaces, warm with sunlight. The big factory windows are open, and a murmur of traffic floats up from the street. You sit on a modernist chaise longue and look around. There is a neat kitchen area, with hanging copper pots. There is a white screen with lights in front of it, and a camera on a tripod. There is a weight set in one corner, two benches, a punching bag and rowing machine. A four-poster bed hung with mosquito netting. There are no nude pictures anywhere, no pornography on the coffee table, just glossy books on architecture. The room smells of freshly ground coffee.

"Coffee?" he says, sitting down. He crosses his legs and you notice his leather sandals, which are like the sandals of little boys in your English childhood.

"No thanks." You are already too nervous.

"Anything else? Soda?"

"No thanks."

"Sure? Not even a glass of wine?"

You look at your watch. "Well."

"I have a bottle of white in the fridge. It's quite good, actually."

"Only if you're sure it's *cold*."

He laughs and gets up. He brings a silver ice bucket back to the coffee table, and two glasses. The bucket is misty with condensation. He pours an almost clear Orvieto into the glasses.

You say, "I love your sandals."

"Thank you." He looks down at them. "I got them because –" He suddenly looks a little shy. "I guess they reminded me of sandals I had when I was a –"

"When you were a kid! That's so –"

"You had them too?"

16

"No, but. The boys I had a crush on always did."

"Really? *Really*? I thought no one else had them. They're rather dweeby, aren't they?"

"Exactly. Sexy dweeby."

He laughs, then grows businesslike again. He takes out a clipboard and writes down your name and some notes which you can't see. He asks you about your experience, about your schedule.

The wine is headache-cold, crisp as lemons. It tastes like spring. A breeze through the huge window makes you shiver. You are drinking too fast.

"So," he says, "do you have any questions?"

"Yes. What do you do with the photographs?"

"Nothing. I put them in a book and look at them. If I gather enough that I like, I'll try to get a gallery show of them. But I'll ask you then if you want to be included. You don't have to sign a release form now, if that's what you're worried about."

"Oh, I'm not worried." You cross your legs. "About anything." You lean forward to hold out your empty glass with him, and you note his quick glance at your legs, down your dress. Finally.

He refills your glass and stands quickly. "So," he says. "Shall we try a few?"

He leads you to a bare square of hardwood floor, and stands you about six feet from the open window. You are in sunlight. He moves around you with his camera, shooting your face, close up, and your head and shoulders. He tells you not to smile. He is very precise in his directions, telling you to move your head exactly so, your gaze exactly here. Then he moves back and sets up his tripod. He takes your photo against the light which you know is filtering through your thin dress, making it diaphanous. At one point a gust blows your skirt up for a second, and you instinctively hold it down.

He asks you to push off the straps of your dress, and he takes your neck and shoulders. You hold the dress to your chest, feeling hot and itchy, hoping he will ask you to drop it. The wine is in your muscles now, making them lazy. You feel like dancing on the shiny floor, or lying down naked in the sun.

But he tells you, crisply, to pull the straps back up. Then he seems to be concentrating on your legs, and the shadows they cast on the floor. You are watching him closely, to see if he seems at all excited, but he appears very serious, constantly re-checking his light meter and his focus.

Then he tells you in the same voice to lift up your skirt a little, so he can see more of your thighs. You do it slowly, watching him. He clicks away. You swing the skirt so the fabric caresses your thighs. You lift the skirt higher, so your white panties are exposed.

"Good," he says quietly. He takes a couple of shots and then says, "Okay, drop the skirt. And then remove the underwear, please."

Awkwardly, you step out of your panties, and then kick them to one side. You notice his eyes following them briefly.

"Lean back against that wall. Good. I want your bottom half in the light and the top in shadow. Good. Now I'm only taking you from the waist down." He shifts the tripod closer.

Leaning against the wall, you are breathing quickly. With him staring so intently through the lens at your middle, at the waist of the thin dress, you feel pinned there. Your thighs rub together.

"Now lift up the dress."

Shyly, you lift the dress. Your thighs come into view, and your little black tuft. Cool air touches you from the window. You lean your head back against the wall, and the camera clicks.

"Good," he says. "Okay. Thank you. That's it for today."

You drop the dress, disappointed. You watch him closely. Perhaps his face is a little bit red. He too has points of sweat on his forehead. But he has been in the square of sunlight too. You watch his arms bulge as they fold up the tripod, and you wonder if anyone has ever made him expose his skin to the camera. You pick up your panties, dust them off and slip them on. His back is politely turned.

He pays you and says, "Well. Thank you. I'll develop these and then I'll call you. You are interested in coming back, if I . . ."

"If you decide you like me?"

"Well, no. No that's not it. It's just that some people, no matter how beautiful in the flesh, don't come out well on film. But I can tell already that you will. I'm sure I'll be calling you. So you are interested?"

"I'll have to think about it. I'll let you know."

"Oh. All right."

You shake his hand and step out into the humid day.

You are sleepy when you get home, from wine and heat. You strip and fall into the cool sheets. You know what you are going to do. You dip your fingers into your sex, which is already wet. You caress the lips, feeling them open on their own. You bring the slickness up to your sensitive point. You gasp and swell. The nub emerges from its hood, yearning. You ache between the legs. It only takes a few touches, a soft flicking back and forth, for the swelling to break, the contractions to begin. Sweat breaks on your forehead, trickles on your neck. You are perfectly silent, clenching your teeth and shuddering in your dim room, as wave after wave breaks in your body. It is short and violent and silent.

Then you fall into a deep, damp sleep, in which you dream of childhood, airports and beaches.

II

All week at work you feel the clients at the restaurant staring at you as if they know that you are a nymphomaniac goddess whore and that you will perform a naked dance for them at any moment, and you smile at all of them, blink your long lashes as if you don't know why they look. You give middle-aged women extra wiggles of your hips as you slide away from their tables; you lean too far forward over the bar to serve underage boys. You wear heels although they kill your feet. (You only try this once; it is not worth it.) You keep tasting the white Orvieto he served you; it must have had something in it. You look in the liquor store for it but can't find it.

You work out obsessively, pressing heavy bars until you sweat, then spending drowsy half-hours in whirlpools and saunas, just touching yourself here and there – your forearm, your chest, your neck – just lightly; no one would notice.

The call comes in exactly a week, after you have taken so many showers and swims you are a perfumed sponge. He wants you this weekend, for about three hours. And he wants you in the same dress, the same everything.

But it is raining on the day. You put a raincoat over your dress and shiver for the streetcar. His studio is washed in grey light. The furniture is dim, with fuzzy edges. Today he wears leather pants, soft and worn but quite tight, and the same sandals, and a ribbed white undershirt like a tank top. It too is tight. He hasn't shaved; he looks a little tougher today.

He gives you the same wine, but you sip it slowly. He puts you in the same place, in front of the window, which is now closed. The only sound in the apartment is the buzzing fridge. He takes the same photographs of your neck, your thighs, your panties with the skirt raised, in the softer light. Then he says, "Take your dress off please."

You pull the dress off over your head and stand, shivering a little, in your underwear. Your hair is still wet.

"And the bra, please."

20

You are excited as you take it off. This is what you were waiting for. He takes close-ups of your goosebumpy breasts and their erect nipples. He makes you lift your hands above your head and gather your hair up, to take the curls on your neck and in your armpits, which you don't shave.

Then he makes you put the bra and the dress back on, and he says, "Come over to the bed please, and lie down."

You tense a little. You are not sure about the bed. But the duvet cover is crisp and white and inviting. At least you are keeping your dress on. You lie on your back, your head propped up by pillows. The sheets smell of detergent, the faint tang of bleach. Hotel sheets.

He is moving the tripod over, shifting lights. He glances at you and says, "Lie on your front, please." He is speaking very softly now.

You roll over, sinking your face into the pillows. Aware that you are wearing no panties, you are keeping the dress pulled down and your legs tight together, your ankles crossed.

He says, "Raise your bum."

You arch your back and bend your knees, lifting your ass in the air. You feel the skirt rising up. You wonder how much of your crack he can see, whether your cheeks are pink or pale in the grey afternoon light.

He sits on the bed, leaning over you, smiling. He rests his hand in the small of your back. You can smell the leather of his pants, and, faintly, his own smell, a whiff of sweat. He wears no cologne. You turn your head to look up at him, uncertainly, but you know that you want him to touch you. You want to reach out and touch his shiny thigh, the ribbed cotton over his chest, his stubbly face. You stay still and tense.

He says in a throaty voice, "You're so beautiful." His hand is stroking your back, smoothing the flimsy skirt over your buttocks.

You raise your ass higher, uncross your ankles. Your breathing is coming faster. You feel the swelling between your legs.

He lifts the skirt up to your waist. You feel his hand brush your naked buttocks. You quiver, tense, grab the sheets with your fists, waiting for his fingers on your sex.

Then he stands and backs off. "Hold it," he says. "Don't move."

Your face is buried in the pillow. You can't see what he's doing. Your back is arched, your ass raised in the air, your skirt around your waist, your legs spread, your lips visible, probably swollen, probably glistening slightly, your asshole visible – this is the position you sometimes take alone, you have imagined this, you know what it looks like, how raw and startling it looks. You are completely open to him now.

You hear the camera making its neat slicing sound, as the shutter blinks and shuts, blinks and shuts.

You want to shock him further. You realize with surprise what you want to do. You don't know why. You can't believe yourself. You can't stop yourself; you reach around with your hand and start caressing your buttocks. The camera stops its clicking. Softly, you run your fingertips over your puffy lips. You realize that you knew all along it would come to this, that this is what you want to do. You feel the wiry hair, the rubbery skin. You push a little harder and the lips split open. You feel them slick inside; the moisture seeps out onto the outer lips as you pull your fingertip up and down, the length of the opening. You know you must be glistening now, to his eye. You smear your wetness up onto your asshole. Your fingers delve into your sex, two at a time, emerging wet and shining. You finger your asshole, and begin to whimper a little into the pillow. You wiggle your hips as your finger plunges into your asshole, slowly, up to the first knuckle, then the second.

The camera clicks. You are shocked and horrified at yourself, amazed by how aroused you are by this crudeness, this total exposure. You feel completely free; it feels like smashing glass, the same delight at the danger, the disintegration. You picture yourself flying, flying through dissolving windowpanes.

You want to know if it is arousing him.

You roll over, your hand still between your legs, to look at him. He sits on a chair beside the bed, his elbows on his knees, leaning forward. He is watching you intently. He smiles, leans back. You see the shining bulge in his leather pants; you see that he is breathing quickly.

You smile at him, your eyes half closed, and spread your legs. You begin to stroke yourself gently, flicking at your clit with soft fingers, then back to stroking your shining lips. Every so often you slide your fingers into your opening, slowly drawing them in and out. Your breathing grows rapid, your eyes close. You begin to moan a little. You know he is staring at your sex, now wide open and glistening, your shining fingers as they slip in and out. You begin to rub your clit harder now, and you feel the warmth spreading through your torso, the muscles in your belly and your ass tensing.

22

Your throw your head back. You are whimpering now, your pelvis jerking up and down. You bring your other hand under your ass, reach up from behind and plunge your fingers into your open sex. You plant your heels on the mattress and raise your pelvis off the bed, rubbing frantically now; you can feel that your clit has emerged from its hood, raw and pink; perhaps he can see it.

You slip one finger into your asshole, you slide it in and out. You can feel the contractions coming now, your leg muscles are shuddering. Your finger on your clit buzzes back and forth so fast you can no longer feel it. You feel a great heat approaching, waves of naked, humiliating pleasure, as intense as pain. You grit your teeth and shriek. You toss your head from side to side. Your legs snap shut, you writhe and contort on the rumpled duvet, convulsing. "Christ," you hear yourself yelling, "oh Christ."

After it passes you have no idea how long it lasted. You lie foetal on the bed, panting, your hair matted to your forehead and neck. You wipe away the tears on your cheeks and lift your head to look at him. He is standing now, his mouth open and his eyes shining. His face glows; there are beads of sweat on his forehead. He steps to the bed and lies on it with you, wraps his arms around you. He strokes your hair, unplasters it from your neck. He kisses your eyes, your neck; he turns you lightly in his hands and kisses the small of your back. You feel his cock hot and hard through the leather against your thigh. He is cupping your breasts, peeling off the fabric of your dress from your damp shoulders.

He kisses your chest, between the breasts, runs his tongue over your hard nipples. You are still quivering a little; you feel sensitive, raw. He is kissing your belly, progressing downward, sliding his hand up your thigh towards your damp groin when you stop him. "No," you say.

He stiffens. "I'm sorry." He drops his hand, props himself up on one elbow. "I shouldn't have . . . I should have asked . . ."

"Just wait a minute." You lie back, look at him, stroke his hair. You trace the line of his stubbly jaw, the sharp lines around his chest muscles. You smile. "I want something else first."

"First?"

"Yes. First. I want to know something."

"Yes."

"People, attractive people, are always exposing themselves to you."

23

"Yes."

"It's very exciting."

"For them or for me?"

"For both."

"Yes." He smiles.

"And," you say lazily, pressing the flat of your palm against the hard ridges in his belly, "you understand why it's exciting to do this . . . for me, I mean, to strip, to expose myself to you."

"Yes. I do. It's exciting because you are beautiful. You are the object of desire. And because . . . because it's releasing to show your sex, I don't mean your sex the part of your body your sex, I mean your sexuality, the fact that you have a sex, that you touch yourself, and to know that you can do that here, without . . ."

"Yes?"

"Without shame. Without judgement." He coughs.

"Yes." You smile. "You understand. You understand so well it makes me wonder, wonder if you, if you have ever . . ."

"Yes?" He is beginning to blush now.

"Done it yourself. Been on the other side of the camera."

"No. But I would like to."

"I thought so."

"I fantasize about it all the time."

Abruptly, you sit up and pull the straps of your dress back up. You pull the skirt down over your knees. "Stand up," you say.

III

He hesitates, smiling as if you are joking.

"Stand up," you order, more crisply.

He stands by the bed, awkwardly, his hands hanging. His cock is clearly outlined in his leather pants; it stands straight up like a bar. He bends slightly at the waist as if to hide it.

You giggle a little and stand up. "Over here, please." You direct him to the white paper backdrop, where the lights are set up. You stand behind his big camera with its long bellows, and puzzle for a moment over the knobs on the heavy tripod. You have not seen a camera like this since film school. You loosen the joints on the legs and slide the camera down to your eye height. "Where's the light meter?"

As you say this you see it hanging around his neck on a string. You hold out your hand. He hands it to you and says, "You know how to use this?"

You smile. "Stay quiet please." You take a reading on his face, and again on the white of his tank top, while he stands with his arms folded, an amused expression on his face. You go back to the camera and set your aperture, your shutter speed. You look at him through the large viewfinder. He is looking a little bored now; his cock has relaxed again. "Stand like that, with your arms folded." You snap him like that, looking defiant, in his leather pants and his white tank top, his taut arms bulging a little as he wraps them around himself. The lights on either side of the set are electronically connected to the camera; they flash with a puffing sound as you push the trigger. "Turn a little to the side, that's right, then look at me. Good. Put your hands on your hips. Spread your feet a little. Tilt your head. No, the other way. Good." You are enjoying controlling him, turning him any way you want. "Now take off your top."

You snap him as he is lifting the undershirt over his head, his stomach muscles flexing. You snap him as he is unbuttoning his leather jeans, exposing a trail of hair up the bottom curve of his belly, the top of his underpants. Now he stands in black fitted shorts, his hands on his hips, looking nervous again.

You stand beside the big camera, considering him from all angles. You stare at his crotch, and it stirs slightly. "Off with your shorts."

He pulls off his shorts, steps out of them. His cock hangs, only slightly swollen, long; the head is already protruding, slightly redder than the rest. It looks undecided. As you begin to take pictures, you see it slowly firming up, growing, until it is sticking almost straight out. His face is flushed. It is getting hot in the studio.

You stop. "You're very athletic," you say.

He shrugs.

"What kind of exercises do you do? I want to see them."

"Like weights?"

"No. I want you to do pushups for me."

He shrugs again. "Okay."

"Down on the floor, please."

He kneels, then lies on the floor, trapping his cock under him. Every time he pushes off from the floor, his cock springs free, and every time he lowers himself it brushes against the floor at its most sensitive point. He grunts with every exertion. You take pictures of him at the top of each pushup, his cock pointing straight down like a pole balancing him in the air. You giggle a little. His shoulders and arms are bulging, shining with sweat; his whole body is taut. His cock grows harder and harder with every touch of the floor; he seems to be throwing himself down more forcefully now, as if slapping it against the floor excites him. Suddenly he collapses, breathing hard.

"Okay," you say, "sit-ups. Go."

He rolls onto his back, draws his knees up, and begins doing sit-ups, his cock waving and swollen, his abdomen rippling and gleaming. You can smell his sweat in the air. Your groin is beginning to tingle again; something about putting this man through his paces, exhausting him for your amusement, is exciting you. You snap him as he pulls his shoulders upwards; you snap him as he lies back down, his body stretched and his cock spiking up from him, swaying as he breathes.

"All right," you say, when he is clearly out of breath. "Lie on your front."

He lies on his front on the white paper floor, his head on his arms, breathing heavily, and you pull the tripod behind him to photograph his sculpted buttocks; they are firm and round as stone globes. You make him roll one way and another.

26

You rub your groin slightly through your dress. Your crotch seems inflamed. "All right," you say, trying to keep your voice even, though your breathing is shallow. "You may stand up."

He stands up and instinctively covers his crotch with his hand, trapping his cock up against his belly.

"Stop. Stand like that. Holding it."

As you take pictures, he suddenly lets go, puts his hands on his hips. His cock springs free, straining upwards, the head swollen, red and shiny. He looks you in the eyes, proudly. Then you notice his eyes are roving over your body, hungrily. He stares at your breasts behind their thin fabric, your bare thighs below the short skirt.

Delicately, he circles the head of his cock with thumb and forefinger. Lightly, he caresses upwards. He gasps a little. You raise your eyes from the head of his cock, and lock with his. He smiles a little, his lips parted.

You look away, busy yourself with the camera. You watch him through the lens as he strokes himself, his finger and thumb grasping tighter now, just below the head of his cock, pulling up then back down in a relentless rhythm. His legs are shaking; he plants his legs wider to steady himself.

With one hand on the camera, you reach down with the other hand and lift up your dress.

He stares at your bush as he strokes. He begins to moan a little. His back arches; his mouth is wide open now, he is panting. He reaches with his free hand to grab a light pole. He leans against it, his face contorted, staring at your exposed sex as if he could fuck it with his eyes, his pelvis jerking as he strokes himself.

You are growing almost as excited as he is; you want to touch your clit but it would mean dropping your hem and obscuring his view, and he seems to be taking so much pleasure in it. You are waiting for the big moment, your finger on the camera button, to capture him.

"Ah," he is saying, from deep in his throat. "Ah. Ah. Diana."

"Yes."

"Diana." His knuckles are white around the light pole.

"Darling," your voice catches, you are rubbing your self with your thumb knuckle as you hold up the hem of your dress, your knees quivering. "Yes. Do it."

"I'm going to, I'm going to –"

27

"Yes. Do it. Come for me. Do it."

His whole fist grips his cock now, as he rubs furiously, quickly, his stomach tight, his shoulders hunched, his chest glistening. The head of his cock is deep purple. "Yes. I'm going to. Ah. Oh my God. Oh fuck. I'm going to. Diana. I'm going to."

"Yes. Darling. Yes."

"Oh fuck. I'm – Diana – I'm – oh fuck. Ah. Ah." He shudders, his knees shake, his pelvis jerks. A white dribble appears at the head of his cock. You press the button, the camera clicks just as the sudden stream appears. He shoots it out over the white paper in two quick jets, then a third, then a fourth. "Oh," he is moaning. "Oh."

He sinks to his knees. The white paper is splattered with his drops. He pants, moans, still pulling on his cock, more gently now. It dribbles a few more drops of milky seed onto his thighs. "Oh my God."

You snap him again as he kneels on the wet paper, exhausted and pink. Then you go to him, kneel and put your arms around his shoulders.

He is still shaking. He kisses you in your neck, and the touch of his warm lips is like a burn on your skin. You cradle his shrinking penis in your hand, spreading its stickiness over your palm.

You both stand, embracing, and he kisses you deeply, sticking his tongue in your mouth. You grasp both his hard buttocks with your hands. He grasps yours, pulling your dress up so he can hold your naked skin. You feel his thigh between your legs and rub against it, hard, feeling your breathing accelerate.

"Come," he says, and backs towards the bed.

He spins you around so you fall backwards onto it and he kneels over you, pulling up your dress. You put your arms over your head so he can pull it off. He falls on you, the two of you naked together, and you feel his chest against your hard nipples, his thigh between your legs. He is kissing your neck, your chest, your breasts. He stretches out your arms, then pins them down, so that he can take your nipples lightly between his teeth while you writhe.

You try to rub your crotch harder against his thigh but he moves it away, then slowly begins kissing down the middle of your belly. You try to stay still as he releases your arms and grabs your hips. He begins to nibble your sex, just lightly licking the outside of your lips, then the inside of your thighs. His strong hands reach under your buttocks and clasp you there, lifting your hips off the bed. His tongue begins to probe your sex, parting your lips, darting in and out. You moan, spread your legs wide; you want his tongue deep in you, you want this pressure released.

His tongue darts in and out, then lightly caresses your clit, your sensitive point, still slightly raw from all your rubbing; it aches and tingles and throbs. Lightly, lightly he licks it, flicking back and forth, then up and down, then in tiny circles, to feel your response.

When he hits on the circles you start to pant in earnest. Your moans come faster, your stomach and your buttocks clench. You feel the warmth approaching from a long way away, and you wriggle your hips as if swimming towards it.

It is as if you are swimming against a thick current, for you feel it growing close and then receding again. Your sex is aching, your clit sensitive from having come so recently, and you clench your teeth as you ride the fine pain towards the pleasure. You feel trapped by his insistent tongue, piercing and probing, and by his iron hands grasping your ass from underneath.

You feel his fingers stroking your sex from below, then one slides gently into your asshole, effortlessly, for you are slick with your juices and sweat there, and at the sensation of this tiny wiggling inside you the gates are opened; you feel the contractions coming slow and long, the waves of release in your body. "Oh God," you are wailing, "oh God."

He licks and sucks until your shuddering has barely subsided, and then slides his body up to be atop yours; he takes your head in his hands and stares fiercely into your eyes. He is wriggling his hips between yours, and you feel the head of his cock, newly stiff again, touch your sensitive opening. You spread your legs, eager for his entry, and then you suddenly realize he is not wearing a condom, and that you hardly know him. "Wait!" you shout, wriggling free from under him, "wait, condom, condom." You grab his shoulder and kiss him on the lips. "Please."

Grinning, he rolls over and pulls on a drawer in the bedside table. He fumbles with the slippery wrapper, tears at it with his lips and spits out the plastic. He is about to place the ring over his cock when you stop him and take it from him. "Let me."

Gently you grasp the base of his cock, then place the ring over the head. Slowly you roll down the flimsy rubber, making sure to stroke the shaft as you go. He grimaces, flinches a little; the head of his cock must still be sensitive.

When it is rolled down you hold his cock to admire it for a second, shining in its plastic coat, the rosy head throbbing in your hand. Then you roll onto your back and he rolls on top of you.

You cry out again as he pushes his way inside you, scratching at his back; as his cock splits you open the waves return, your orgasm continues, your entire skin feels like a sex organ, as if every touch will make you come and come again.

He is sliding in and out, deep, now, having raised himself on his palms, and he is staring into your eyes with his teeth clenched as he pounds. You shudder and cry with every slam of his cock inside you, your rawness and your pleasure mixed together into an unbearable buzzing, and you continue to shriek, "Yes, oh, yes, oh, fuck, fuck me, oh, Christ, oh fuck, oh no, oh no." It seems you will never stop coming, your muscles seem locked in perpetual spasm.

He lies down on you now with his full weight, kissing and biting your neck, and reaches under you to grab your ass again, so as to plunge deeper and harder into you. His hips jerk faster and faster, and he is silent except for his heavy breathing. You realize he is slow to come, having come, like you, just minutes before.

He slows, withdraws, and briskly turns you over. You bury your face in the pillow, clench the sheets with both fists, and wait for his entry. But he doesn't plunge right in; he grabs you by the hips and pulls upwards, pulling you onto your hands and knees.

He pushes his cock inside you, and begins his slow thrusting. It is deeper this way, and you feel the tip of his cock brushing against the front of the inside of your sex and moan again. He accelerates his thrusting, and you shudder with every jerk. Then you feel his hands on your shoulders, pushing you down. He wants you to plant your face in the bed, just as you had posed him for the camera.

You lower your head and shoulders to the pillow, stretching your arms out to either side, totally helpless now against his furious thrusting, your ass in the air. You know he is looking down on you, holding onto your hips, controlling your movement, the globes of your ass quivering with every thrust, your asshole open and exposed, and you can feel this exciting him. He is grunting now as he slams into you, harder and faster, and you feel his cock wiggling slightly inside you, until suddenly he slows, stops his thrusting, and lets out a low wail like air escaping, his cock jerks and jerks inside you as it spurts, and he collapses on top of you, sweating and heaving.

His cock slips out, and you roll to take him in your arms. You lie quivering together, kissing softly. You take his tender penis gently in your hand, where it curls and sleeps. He cups your breasts in his palms, pushes your wet hair from your eyes.

"No one has ever done that for me before," he says finally. "I mean made me pose like that."

"You mean done that *to* you."

"Yes. No one has ever done that to me. Or for me."

"No one has ever done that for *me*," you say. "Posed for me, I mean."

The watery light from the factory windows is dimming, a soft, rainy summer light.

He kisses your eyelids. "You're hired, by the way," he murmurs. "As a model. You're a very good model."

You say, "I hope the pictures turn out."

IV

And so begins your relationship with Patrice. You start to spend every morning in the studio, before your shift, and he takes your photograph and you take his, and then you make love.

It's a mysterious life, though. You don't know what he does when you're not with him. You don't know if you're the only visitor to the studio. You begin to look around the studio, surreptitiously, for evidence of other models, other photographs. You find none.

Once you arrive to find someone in the studio with him: a young man, a young black man with a shaved head and shining muscles. They are sitting together drinking coffee, laughing. He introduces him as Clarence. You are suddenly jealous of this friend's beauty – until Patrice poses you together, you with your white dress on, Clarence naked, shining and muscular, kneeling at your feet, his hands lightly circling your thighs, his nose brushing against them as Patrice turns you this way and that. You know that from where he is kneeling, Clarence can see up your skirt to your panties – they are only plain ones today, white cotton: you wish you had worn something gauzy or silky. You glance at his penis, solid and thick, only slightly swollen, lifting slowly and cautiously as he brushes your thighs with his fingertips. Patrice tells you to put one foot on Clarence's head. Clarence bows his head, docile, for the heel of your shoe. You breathe in his clovey smell and look down at the penis as it swells and lengthens. You want the bulb of the penis to grow large, to circle it with your fingers, then to feel it inside you.

But Patrice does not let things go this far. He does not let you take off your dress. He photographs you with Clarence behind you, Clarence's hands wrapping around and cupping your breasts. He asks you to throw your head back. Clarence kisses your exposed neck. You feel the touch of his teeth on your vulnerable skin. You feel Clarence's penis against your ass, hard and upright. You rub against it. And then Patrice stops, tells Clarence to get dressed. You sigh, but you are relieved. You don't want Clarence, you want Patrice.

You are waiting for Patrice to pose you with a woman. You know he

32

wants to, to watch you together, and you don't know how you will feel about it, whether you will be disgusted or aroused, whether you will be jealous.

Patrice tells you he wants to take you to a strip club. He wants to see if you will be aroused by all the naked female flesh. You want to go, too: you have always been curious about these closed places, with their false windows and their crude signs, the places where boyfriends go when they don't want their girlfriends, their apartments, their cats. Where boyfriends go to become other people. You imagine them all gathering in there, ordering beers, and then peeling off their masks, like aliens in a science fiction movie, to reveal God knows what hairy, fanged faces.

You are more curious to see if Patrice will be aroused than to know if you will be. You are pretty sure you won't be. Although you want to know how beautiful the girls are. Just so you know.

You must pass a bouncer to enter the bar, a bald man in a white shirt who opens the door for you without registering any surprise on his face as he looks you up and down. "Good evening, folks," is all he says. Even though it is only four in the afternoon. But it is always night, it seems, in a strip club. You climb a staircase whose steps are carpeted with red velvet and lined with rows of tiny lightbulbs. It reminds you of discos in movies from childhood. There is loud dance music playing.

Inside, the bar is so dark you both stand for a moment, blinking. There is a black light somewhere, glowing purple, making every patch of white clothing stand out like a ghost. There are bars of neon blinking at you from around the stage. A strobe light flashes. The music throbs. There is a heavy sweet smell, something like incense: you realize it is the night-club smell of the smoke machines, billowing mist out onto the stage, the smell of burning mineral oil.

The forms in the room are just shadows: men in clumps, at tables along the front of the stage. You take Patrice's arm, stand very close to him. You make out the figures of waitresses circulating in the gloom, all half-naked, it seems: girls in tight shorts, in ultra-short miniskirts, in glowing white bras. In the black light their skins all seem deeply tanned, their hair all jet black. They all wear heels like steeples, making their legs look long and slim and perfect, all of them. A stripper passes, naked except for a white thong that glows as it glides past as if walking on its own. You swallow quickly. The sweet smell of the smoke is Eastern; the nudity like a medieval fantasy. This is like a harem.

The stripper is carrying a plastic stool which she places in front of a man sitting alone at a low table; a young man, in a suit, with his briefcase sitting at his face. She kneels on it and pushes her naked breasts right into his face. He sits totally motionless. You are astounded at the openness of it, at how close she gets to him, how calm and nonchalant she seems about it. It makes you feel like a prude. She is smiling and talking to the man, although he does not reply.

Boomba boomba boomba, goes the music. *Sweet dreams are made of this.*

Patrice leads you through the tables. There are table dances going on everywhere, totally naked girls with their long legs draped over the shoulders of motionless men, or wiggling their buttocks inches from their faces. Men turn and raise their eyebrows at you, scowl, then look away. A waitress smiles and winks at you as you pass. You sit in a booth against a mirrored wall. There are mirrors everywhere, but you wonder why, because it is too dark to see anything in them except the kaleidoscopic reflections of coloured lights and strobes.

There is a lithe woman on the stage, clinging to the pole. She is wearing sharp heels and a pair of thong-back panties. She tosses her long brown hair, writhes against the pole. You stare at her intensely, suddenly unaware of anything but her perfect body. Her breasts are brown spheres, perfectly round and firm. You wonder if they are real; you have not seen enough fake ones to tell. The woman is a girl; she must be nineteen or twenty, or even younger, although you know that would be illegal. Her skin is utterly unblemished, her face lovely.

You are surprised. You don't know why you expected the women in a strip club to be haggard and cheap looking, but you did.

The dancer on the stage is teasing the men in the front row now, slipping her fingers inside the waistband of her panties, tugging them down on her hips an inch, then up again. She pulls them down to reveal just a wisp of pubic hair, then lets the waistband snap into place, and begins her dancing again. The men are whistling and jeering at her. She turns her back to them and bends over, low, so her ass is in the air, wiggling. She grasps her ankles and smiles at the crowd from between her legs, upside down.

You look over at Patrice, who is ordering your drinks from another beautiful waitress. Honestly, all the women in here look like models. You

34

feel small. You try to sink into the back of the booth, where you will not be seen. But the waitress catches your eye and smiles. "How are you?" she mouths in the noise. "Drink?" You smile back, wondering why she does not see you as a threat in this place. Perhaps she just wants you to know she's not a threat to you. You order a vodka and tonic and watch her walk her hippy swingy high-heel walk through the tables. You wonder how she can walk like that all night.

The stripper on the stage is wriggling out of her panties now, slowly working them down her thighs with her thumbs, spreading out her fingers on either side. Her head is bent forward so that her hair falls around her face; she looks out from under it with a wicked smile. She is sexy, this girl. Something about the way she is taking so much pleasure, or seems to be taking so much pleasure, in that slow progress of the little bit of Lycra and cotton down her smooth thighs makes your crotch tingle for a second; you feel a trouble in your belly. It is not that you lust for her, you don't think; it is that you feel a little of her sexuality in you. You feel, for a second, those mesmerized men's eyes on you.

Patrice leans back, puts his arm around you. He says in your ear, "You want a table dance?" You shake your head vigorously. That would make you nervous. "You get one," you shout.

He shrugs. He raises his hand at one of the strippers leaning against the bar. A small girl in a red silk camisole saunters over, smiling. Her hair is in two cute pigtails. She smiles warmly at both of you, settles her plastic stool in front of Patrice.

"Hi," she says. "I'm Keisha. How are you? Now which one of you is this for?"

"For him," you say quickly, and you point and then tap him on the shoulder, as if to preclude any possible confusion.

She laughs and says "Okay," and raises her eyebrows at Patrice as if to say, *whatever*.

She kneels on her stool, her hands on her hips, and closes her eyes. She begins to sway to the music, just swinging her hips in a circle. Then her hands begin smoothing down the sides of her camisole, passing over her hips and thighs. She lifts the camisole up to reveal her red silk thong. Slowly, she pulls up her top, over her small breasts, over her head. She tosses it away, and arches her back, pushing her little breasts towards Patrice's face, smiling. "I just have little ones," she says, which makes you

35

both smile. She is so proud of them. Patrice's hand twitches as if he is about to reach up and touch them, but he stops himself. He reaches over and takes your hand.

You hold his tightly, glad of the contact.

Keisha strokes her breasts, first with her fingertips, then with her palms, looking Patrice firmly in the eye. Patrice is sitting stiffly upright, his eyes fixed on her breasts. He swallows, grips your hand tighter. Her breasts are shallow and firm, her nipples small. They harden, two dark bullets. You are so close you can see the goosebumps around the aureoles.

She shakes them in his face, leans forward so that his nose is right between them. You wonder if he can smell her skin.

She sits on her stool, points her legs in the air and unclips the side of her panties. They fall open; she slides them off one leg. She points her toes in the air, then swivels so that her feet are in front of Patrice's face. Like a gymnast, she lowers her ankles onto his shoulders. She flexes her knees. Her thighs are wide apart. His eyes are fixed right into her open vagina, right in front of him. You look over her knee to see her cunt. It is neatly trimmed, a strip of hair up the middle. Her little lips are slightly parted. It gives you a shiver. You didn't realize it was going to be so gynecological. She turns, kneels again on the stool, with her back to him. She bends forwards, thrusting her ass in the air, sliding it closer to his face. She sticks her buttocks right in his face. She spreads her knees wider.

Patrice is absolutely still and stiff, gripping your hand tightly. He is staring right into her ass, a half-inch from his nose. You giggle, and muffle your mouth with your hand. Keisha looks behind her and smiles at you. She winks.

She turns and wiggles her breasts in his face some more, rubs her cheek against his, rubs her breasts against his chest. Then, quickly, it is over: she stands up, picks her panties off the floor. Patrice fumbles with his wallet and hands her ten dollars.

She takes it, smiling, then bends over you, wrapping her hand around the back of your neck, and says, "Do you want one?"

You shake your head. "No, thank you."

"Yes," says Patrice. "I want you to. I'll pay."

Keisha is massaging the back of your neck with her hand. "Okay?"

"If you want me to, Patrice."

She kneels on her little stool again, so close she can brush her breasts against yours. She drapes her pigtails on your shoulders, brushes her cheek against yours. You can smell perfume and cigarette on her breath. Your body is alert, tingling, troubled, but perhaps not aroused.

Keisha strips off her silky top, begins massaging her nipples again. You see them grow stiff, and your own grow stiff. You squirm a little in your seat. You don't know what to think of this.

Men are watching, you can tell, discreetly, from a distance. Two of them have even stood up to watch, one booth over. Keisha has closed her eyes and is moaning a little.

You glance over at Patrice. He smiles at you. He takes your hand.

Then, surprisingly, Keisha takes your other hand and places it firmly on her breast. You start, jerking it back as if the touch of the smooth skin burns. In fact, it is cool, cool and firm and taut. You relax, spreading your fingers out over the shallow breast, letting the nipple pop between your fingers. Keisha writhes against you. You have never touched a woman's naked breast before. "I thought I wasn't allowed to touch," you whisper in Keisha's ear.

"*You* are," she purrs, then giggles. "Besides, it turns the other guys on so much. I'll make a pile tonight. Are you enjoying it?"

"Yes."

She turns, pushes her ass in the air, shoves it towards you. This is where you are going to get the full gynecological tour. You can feel tension ripple through the watching men. They shift a little closer to watch. Patrice's hand tightens on yours.

Keisha's ass is so close to your face you can see the puffy lips of her cunt, the bumps where she has shaved. You pull back a little. She is so clean you cannot detect the faintest scent of flesh. You concentrate on her long smooth legs, the perfection of her skin.

She sits on the stool, swings on her ass so she faces you again, puts her ankles on your shoulders. You stare into her open pussy. Lazily, she strokes it, parting the lips a little. Under your dress, you part your own legs a little. You can't help it. You imagine her cunt to be your own. You picture Patrice's hard cock splitting it open, what it must look like from his position. You breathe quickly. Your heart has sped up.

The song ends, and Keisha stands up suddenly. Show over. Patrice hands her another ten dollars, and she ruffles your hair, blows you a kiss, and saunters away, carrying her little plastic stool. You stare at the floor, so as not to catch the men's staring eyes.

"Phew," you say. "I think I want you to fuck me now."

Patrice takes you back to his studio in a taxi. He opens the door and does not turn on the lights; he leads you, in the darkness, straight to the white linened bed, draped in invisible mosquito netting. He pushes you through the netting, fine as spiderwebs, and onto your back. You pull up your dress, over your head and off, you lie back, waiting, while he strips off his clothes. He falls on you, heavy and hard and rough, and you open your legs to feel his thick cock pushing against your crotch, against your panties. His rough-stubbled chin nuzzles your neck, his tongue flicks at your nipples. You writhe together, under the tent of netting, kissing and licking and groping. He reaches down and works your panties down your thighs, roughly. His cock is flat against your lips now, rubbing up and down. You are gasping, "Oh yes, put it in."

He pulls back, lies beside you. You turn to face each other and kiss. He strokes your sides, your thighs, your ass, your breasts, kissing you.

He says, "Have you ever fantasized about being with a man and a woman together?"

You laugh. "No, but I bet you have."

"Of course I have. But I bet you have too. I bet you have. Be honest."

You think for a moment. "I've thought about it, sure. But it's not . . . it's not a big one. A big fantasy."

"Are you thinking about it now?"

You close your eyes and picture the throbbing light of the strip club, the neon pinks and purples, the buzzing beat. You can smell the sweet smoke smell, Keisha's perfume. You picture her taut little nipples. "Yes."

"I want you to imagine something." Patrice turns you onto your back, so he is whispering in your ear. His hand wanders over your breasts, your belly, your groin, just brushing against your skin, always moving. Gently, he parts your legs so he has easy access to your wet lips.

"Am I going to have my first bisexual experience?"

"Yes. A virtual one."

You laugh. His caressing hand is on the verge of tickling you; you writhe and squirm a little, but he does not stop.

"I want you to imagine we are all in a bed together. Me, you and her."

"Yes."

"I am on this side. She is on the other side."

"Yes."

"And she's stroking that breast. While I stroke this one."

"Yes."

"And she's nuzzling your neck with her lips on that side. Like this."

"Mmmm."

"And I have my knee over your leg, like this. And she wraps her leg around you from that side."

"I'm getting all the attention. Do I have to do anything?"

"No. That's the point. We're both here to please you. You just close your eyes. And open your legs."

"Oh."

"And relax."

"Oh my."

"Yes. That's her hand between your legs. And now this is her mouth on your nipple."

"Mmm. That feels good." You feel Patrice's cock hard against your thigh. Your eyes are closed. You are imagining her hot breath on your neck, your breast. The feeling of her little breast squashed against your arm. Her long hair draped over your shoulder. You would like to touch her, too.

Patrice's hand is probing your sex now, thrusting in, then withdrawing and making circles around your clit. You feel the warmth and wetness seeping out. His rough tongue on your nipple.

You imagine feeling the wiry brush of her pubic hair against your thigh. A mouth on each nipple. "Oh," you say. "I think . . ."

"Yes." Patrice's rubbing is firmer now. Your clit is hard and swollen.

"I think I'm going to . . . oh."

"Yes."

"Oh."

"Yes. Yes, Diana. Come. Come."

Your hips jerk; your belly clenches. "Oh God," you say. "I'm coming. Keisha. Keisha. I'm coming."

"Yes. Yes."

You wail and writhe, Patrice's fingers deep inside you, his lips clamped on your nipple.

You feel the contractions passing, your breathing slowing. "God," you say. "Oh God. I love it with women."

Patrice laughs, kissing your face wetly. "That was a fast one. I think you do."

"Now you come." You grab at him, try to pull him on top of you.

He rolls away, opens the drawer in the bedside table. "One second."

You breathe deeply while you watch him roll the condom onto his erect penis. It glistens. He slides on top of you, pins your arms to the bed. You feel the head of his cock pushing big and swollen against your lips. You part your legs to welcome him, but he does not thrust in.

"What about two men?" he says.

"Two men and me? I . . . I haven't thought about that."

"Of course you have."

"Well, yes, I've thought about it, but . . ."

"Did you enjoy it?"

"Oh, I would never *do* it."

"Did you enjoy *thinking* about it?"

You look away from him. "Well, it's a kind of scary fantasy. You don't know what could happen. It could be . . . it could be scary."

"Yes."

"I thought – I thought that's what was going to happen to me when you posed me with that guy. Clarence."

"Yes?" He laughs, releases your hands. He rolls off you, lies at your side. "I would be too jealous to share you with Clarence. He's too good looking."

"Yes. I figured that. But I thought about it, anyway."

"And?"

You nod. "I thought about it. But I wouldn't want to do it in reality. I'm not sure what I'd feel about being a sandwich filling."

"Well, it wouldn't have to be like that. There are other . . . anyway, it doesn't matter. It doesn't have to happen in reality. Nothing bad can happen in your fantasy." He pulls you to him, so you are facing him, lying on your side. He holds one nipple between his fingers, his captive. "What did you imagine? When you thought about it?"

"Well." You take a deep breath. "I would want them to be tender with one another, too. I have a fantasy about seeing boys kiss."

"Really?"

"Mmm. Two really good-looking boys. I want to see them kiss."

He laughs shortly. "Okay. We'll kiss. But we'll touch you, too."

"Oh yes. I'll lie in the middle. The way I did with Keisha." You roll over, onto your back. "And I'll let you both stroke and kiss and touch me."

"Yes."

"And then I'll grab both your cocks." You take Patrice's firm cock in your fist. "And I'll jerk you both at the same time. Up and down."

"Oh."

"Like this."

"Yes. Oh."

"A cock in each hand. I've got you both."

"Oh. Yes. Gently."

"No. Firmly. Like this."

"I'll come."

"No, you won't. I'll stop before you come." You still your hand.

"Jesus." Patrice is panting. "Fuck. I want to come now."

"Yes. You will." You roll towards him, pull him close to you. You lie facing each other, intertwined. "Now I want you in front of me. And him behind me."

"Yes." Patrice is holding you tight and close now. His hands clutch your buttocks. His cock is held between your thighs, throbbing. "He's behind you. Do you feel his cock hard up against your ass?"

You close your eyes. You can really almost feel the warmth of a second man behind you. His cock trapped between your buttocks. You shiver. You are growing excited again.

"And he's wrapping his arms around your front, cupping your breasts. And kissing the back of your neck. While I kiss your mouth. Your lovely throat."

"I want you inside me."

Easily, Patrice thrusts his cock between your wet lips. He fills you. Your sex is tender.

You groan. "Yes."

Slowly, Patrice begins thrusting. His hands around your buttocks, pressing you to him, feel like the hips of the stranger behind you, pressing against you.

Between breaths, Patrice says, "His cock is sliding. Up and down. In the crack of your ass. My cock is pumping. In your pussy."

41

"Yes." You feel Patrice's finger sliding into your asshole. You are so slick it slips in easily.

"Do you want him inside you?"

"No. Yes."

Patrice slips another finger into your asshole. "He's inside you now. We both are."

You are thrusting your hips against Patrice's now, seeking friction. You slide your ass back and feel his fingers in your ass; forward and his cock rams into you. You feel open as an ocean. You feel your sex and buttocks clenching around his cock, his fingers. His groin rubs agains your tender clit. Your body is tightening.

His thrusting comes faster and harder. His fingers go deeper into you. He closes his eyes and frowns, the face he makes when he is about to come.

"Yes," you say, "come before I do."

"No. No. Come with me."

"Oh. Yes. Yes. Fuck me."

"Yes! Yes!" His face is contorted now, red and grimacing. You feel his cock jerk and throb inside you, you feel his back stiffen under your fingertips, as he comes, and you feel yourself coming too, rubbing against him as hard as you can, wrapping your legs around his to squeeze him into you, as if you were squeezing the come out of him and deep into you. "Yes! Yes!" he is yelling, and you yell it too – "Yes! Yes!"

He relaxes and sighs, and you lie together in silence for a long time, feeling the aftershocks pass up and down your bodies in long shudders.

"There," he says finally, lifting strands of wet hair off your face. "Your first sandwich."

You sigh deeply. "I'm not sure I'd really want it, in real life."

"Who said anything about real life? Isn't this good enough?"

"Yes," you say. "Scary, but good. Now you boys kiss each other."

He kisses you roughly, wetly, on the mouth, his tongue probing yours. "See, we can both be girls and boys," he says.

V

And then one evening Patrice telephones you to tell you that he will be going away, the next day. He doesn't know for how long. It is a business trip. You do not ask for more information than that; you are suddenly exhausted and do not want to know. He says he will miss you and will communicate with you; he does not explain how.

A week passes and you feel lost. You are faced once again with the mere drudgery of the Stoic Grill; you remember, as if you have been asleep, that you have nothing else going on. Patrice's absence sobers you, makes you think once again about what you are going to do with your film projects, with your life.

You apply for a job as a story producer on a radio show about the arts. You apply for a job as a junior editor at a fashion magazine. You apply for a job as an assistant to a documentary filmmaker. You do all this without excitement, with a dull sense of obligation, and are amazed and stunned when you are offered each and every one of these jobs, within a space of three days. You must make a panicky decision, faced once again with the troubling realization that you are talented and valuable, that you have an education that is being wasted on the sad regulars at the Stoic Grill (that row of tweedy yet unshaven men at the bar, with their earnest lectures about the global economy, their reminiscences of fishing trips, their planned memoirs, their faintly hostile flirtation), that your mere appearance will probably win you a job.

You take the least important job, the assistant to the film producer, because it is the one you think you are least likely to fail at, and because the filmmaker is a woman, and you like her work, which is about scientific research into human perception, or about gay male painters, depending on her mood, and because you love her office space, in an industrial warehouse downtown, with its shiny wood floors, its dark blue walls, its heavy velvet curtains and paisley throws, its antique office chairs and burgundy chaise longue, where the tabby cat sleeps and stretches, sleeps and stretches all day long.

In your first few days of work, all you do is sit and talk with the film-maker, as she strokes the tabby cat or polishes her spectacles, about gender differences and their basis in physiology. The cat watches you through slit eyes.

You are happy and excited when you are with her. But from the moment you take the subway back to your dim apartment, there is a emptiness in you, a hunger. Patrice has aroused something in you and you cannot repress it. On weekends you wander the city streets without knowing where to go, having lost all your previous patterns. You are horny all the time, craving abandon and titillation, both vulnerability and control. You alternately miss Patrice and hate him for abandoning you.

Then one day at work the fax machine clicks and shudders and a handwritten letter begins to emerge. You see your name on it and tear it out of the machine.

You sit on the burgundy chaise longue and begin to read it and your face grows hot. You realize how lucky your were that your boss was out of the room, in fact out of the office, that you are alone in the dark blue studio with the rainy sky outside and the cat purring beside you.

The letter reads:

D. –

Do you know what I'm going to do to you when I see you again? I'm going to push you against a wall and kiss you hard, on your lips and neck and face and breasts, and I'm going to thrust my tongue into your mouth and cup your breasts in my palms. I'm going to rub my hands all over your thighs and buttocks, clutch your buttocks in my hands and squeeze them like sponges and hold them tight to me so you can feel how stiff my shaft is in my pants, my pelvis pinning you to the wall, my chest tight against yours. And I'm going to push my hand between your legs and cup your mound, press against it firmly so you have to open your thighs, and I'm going to rub against your panties until you gasp and say no, stop, let me lie down, but I won't; I won't let you move or sit down until I feel a wetness seeping through, and then I'll pull the waistband down and slip my fingers into you, holding you up against the wall and kissing your neck wetly, with your hair in my mouth and your hands clutching my back and buttocks. And with my other hand I'll be freeing my belt and yanking my pants down, so that you feel my cock burning hot against your thigh. And I'll stab you, thrust right deep inside you, standing up, pierce you to the pit, and I'll come right away, squirting and throbbing and jerking inside you.

And then I'll let you lie down, and I'll pull your dress off over your head and pull your panties off and lick your nipples, feeling them harden between my lips, and slowly lick down your belly towards your cleft, and then bury my tongue between your folds, all wet and salty, and lick and suck and rub my way up to the little hardening button of your clit, jerking my tongue back and forth until you cry out and clench. And all this time I'll be feeling myself harden again, so that as soon as I feel your waves beginning I'll plunge inside you again, feel you contracting around me, and I'll thrust in and out as hard as I can, making you say, "oh, oh, oh," as you come around me.
P.

There is no date, no place. You study the page to decipher the phone number of the originating fax machine. It is an area code you do not recognize. You cross and uncross your legs, and walk to the big plate glass window of the studio. You look out on the rainy street. There are umbrellas on the sidewalk below, gliding and shifting like canoes on the sluicing street. No one is looking up. You picture the faces under the umbrellas as narrow, furrowed, concentrating on their feet as they pattern the pavement with steps.

You unbutton your cardigan, let it drop to the floor. You unbutton your crisp white businessy blouse. Under it you wear a bra of dark blue lace. You put both palms to the cold window pane. You look up, to the office building across the street. It is dark, ornamented with scrollwork and capitals, Victorian commercial gloom. Its windows are dark. You cannot tell what eyes they hide.

Your studio is dark. The phone is quiet for once. Your boss could walk in at any moment. You slip your blouse off your shoulders. It falls to the floor. You jump as something brushes your calf; you did not hear the cat as it padded across the wood floor. It rubs against your leg, mewling softly. You shiver in the cool air. The fall is coming.

You turn quickly to look at the studio's main door. You hear no sound from the hallway outside. You pull down the lacy cups of your bra so that your nipples pop out, hard in the cool, damp air of the afternoon. You lean forward and press them against the cold glass. You gasp. No one on the street looks up.

You reach behind your back and unclasp your bra. You shake it off. You stretch your arms out and press your whole torso against the wide, pure glass window on the street, exposed to the sky and the shoulders of buildings across the gulf of street, crucified against the glass. You flatten your breasts with their hard nipples, a ring of goosebumps on each aureole, the side of your neck against the hard coldness, shivering. You are aroused.

There is a clatter from the hallway as someone outside fumbles with keys, and you leap back from the window, scooping up your bra, blouse and cardigan and scuttling towards the washroom door. You make it inside just a second before the front door opens and Clara bustles in, singing hello. With shaking hands, you pull on bra and shirt, breathing fast. You have an image flashing on your retinas like a ghost, something you saw from the corner of your eye in the second before you rushed from the window, a white shirt in a window of the building opposite. A man standing in the window across from you, watching. You did not have time to see his face, in the shadow of the Victorian building.

VI

You help your boss, Clara, write a treatment for a documentary film on three fascist painters, and then a treatment for a documentary film about two feminist pornographers. Since both of these proposals attract investors and funding agencies, you are suddenly busy. You must travel regularly with Clara, to meet investors and directors and interview subjects. Clara encourages you to speak at these meetings, to explain the films, as you seem to be able to do it in a more straightforward way than she can. You speak to producers every day. She gives you a cellphone and asks you to go on research trips on your own. She seems to be treating you as an equal. You look at yourself in the mirror and say the word "producer" and giggle.

You are in a carpeted reception area in an office tower in Vancouver when your cellphone rings. You answer briskly.

"I'm in a hotel room," says a male voice. A faint French accent.

"Patrice. Patrice." You stand and look out the tinted window at the mountains, the glittering harbour. You hold the collar of your blouse closed as if you were suddenly naked. "Patrice. Where are you?"

"I told you. In a hotel room."

"Where?"

"I'm standing at the window."

"No, where —"

"Listen. I'm wearing my leather pants. But I have no shirt on."

You are silent, feeling your breathing accelerate. Your face is flushed. You glance over to the receptionist. She is talking on the phone; she appears not to see you.

Patrice's voice is low and gravelly. He sounds so close he is whispering in your ear. "I have a hard-on. I'm so excited." His voice is shaky.

"Yes," you say. You feel pain and longing for Patrice, but you know, somehow, you cannot tell him this, or you will lose this moment. You will lose this arousal.

"I've bought this . . . this thing." He laughs a little.

"What thing?"

"It's this cock ring thing. But it's also a vibrator."

47

"Yes."

"It's a ring with a vibrator on it, so it goes around your cock and . . . it just vibrates."

Softly, you say, "At the base?"

"If you wanted. If I were fucking you −" His voice catches. "For example. I would wear it at the base. With the little vibrating egg. On the." His breathing is rapid. "Top. And every time I pushed into you, it would push against your clit. And buzz against it."

"Yes." You glance over at the secretary. She is staring at her computer screen, talking on her phone. There is no one else in the reception area. You can see through the glass walls into the office; you can see the man you are waiting to see in his glass cubicle. He is sitting at his desk, in his charcoal suit, looking into his computer screen, talking on his phone. His face is red. You wonder if he is having phone sex. Maybe everyone in the office, the secretary and everybody, is having phone sex. You turn back to the window, look out at the city towers through the blue glass. Blue clouds are seeping over the sky.

"And," says Patrice, "I would push my cock inside you and you would feel it throbbing there, and I would just hold it there, hold it still, squeezing the vibrator part against your clit. I would hold it there until you . . ."

"Yes." Without moving your body, facing the window, you slip your hand into a gap in your blouse. You lay your palm flat against the warm skin of your belly. The top of your hand brushes against the lace of your bra. "Yes. Do you have it on your cock right now?"

"Just a minute." You hear a zipper. "I'm stepping out of my pants."

"Are you still standing in the window."

"Yes."

"So am I."

"Are you in public?"

"Yes. I'm waiting for a meeting."

"Are you touching yourself."

"Yes."

"So am I. I'm putting the vibrating ring on. It's tight. It pinches your skin."

You hear a faint buzzing over the phone line. "Is it on?"

"Yes."

"Are you hard?"

"Very."

"Where is the vibrating part right now? Is it around the base?"

"I have it. The ring. Right up around the top of my cock. Around the head. It's tight around the head. So that the head is all. All."

"All what?"

"Swollen. It's purple."

"Yes. I wish I could see it." You press yourself as close to the window as you can. You cup your breast with your palm. You hope it appears from behind that you are merely hugging yourself or scratching yourself.

"The vibrating part is. Under. On the underside. Right on the sensitive. Oh."

"Yes."

"But when I push it into you. I have it on top, so it's buzzing against your clit. I have you tied up. So you can't fight the. I hold it there."

"Yes."

"With my cock inside you. Deep."

"Throbbing," you murmur.

"And I'll wait. Holding you down. Your legs are spread and tied down. And I won't let up. Pushing the buzzer against you, even if you try to, try to move away. I have you pinned. Until you come against the . . . against the vibrator. Oh."

"Yes." You cradle the cellphone against your shoulder. You steady yourself against the window with one hand, the other hand cupping your breast. You stand with your legs tight together, your ankles crossed. Your face is flushed; you feel hot. You do not dare to turn around to look at the secretary. A seaplane is making an approach to the harbour.

"And I'll wait until you come and then I'll. Spurt inside you. You'll feel it . . . . I'm. I'm."

"Are you coming now?" you whisper. "In the window?"

"Yes," he gasps. "It's coming. It's. Fuck. Jesus. Fuck."

"Ms Artemis?" calls the secretary.

You pull your hand out from inside your blouse. "Patrice," you whisper. "I have to –"

"Oh," he is moaning. "Oh God. Fuck. Diana. Oh."

You turn around, smiling at the secretary. "Yes?"

"Mr MacArthur's ready for you now."

"Great. Be right there."

Patrice's moaning has subsided. You just hear his heavy breathing.

"Patrice? I have my meeting now."

He whimpers.

"But tell me where you are and I'll –"

He whispers, "Goodbye, my love." And disconnects.

You fold up the cellphone, put it into your briefcase as calmly as you can. Your hands are shaking. You walk towards Duncan MacArthur's glass cubicle on unsteady legs.

He pushes his rolling chair back and stands and extends his meaty hand in one gesture. "Diana. Diana, I'm so glad to meet you."

"Hi." You are still breathing rapidly. Perhaps Duncan MacArthur will think you are excited to see him.

"Have a seat."

You notice he keeps glancing at your chest, and then you realize that the top two buttons of your blouse are open and showing two lacy semicircles. Your hand darts up; you are about to close the button but instead you just touch your neck lightly, let your fingers slide over your chest. You don't know why you hesitate. Perhaps you are enjoying Duncan MacArthur's eyes on your chest. He seems mesmerized by your fingertips, their light caressing. You are still hearing Patrice's voice as he comes. *Oh. Oh.* You shudder, cross your legs. Your miniskirt rides up on your thighs but you don't care. Your skin feels hot; you want to cool it off.

He jerks his eyes up to yours. "So. Had a good flight?"

"Oh," you murmur, speaking as softly as you can. "Tiring."

"Yeah. That's the . . . that's the thing." He seems to be trying hard not to drop his eyes to your chest again. "I'm really glad you could come all this way. I, ah, I don't know if you're aware, I'm sure you know that I've worked with your partner before, Clara, yeah, of course you know, terrific woman, terrific director, and we just heard about this project and we thought we'd at least, at least like to ah . . ." His eyes drop again. He leans forward, his eyes wide and excited, his face anxious and questioning. "To touch base."

You lean back in your chair as Duncan MacArthur talks. You glance around the office. There is one wall of windows, one real wall, and two glass walls separating them from the rest of the office. The divider walls have venetian blinds covering them. You could just reach over and twist the rod behind Duncan MacArthur and the blinds would close, leaving the office dim. You picture yourself leaning forward, across the desk, as Duncan MacArthur talks so nervously, leaning as if to kiss him but just reaching out over his shoulder to grasp control of the blinds, your face just beside his head as he stops talking suddenly, startled by your shoulder brushing his face, your scent and hair in his nose, your blouse hanging open before his eyes, billowing open to reveal your little breasts in their lacy filigree, the smooth skin between them. You would close the blinds and lean back again, watching him. And slowly you would hike your skirt up.

"Don't you think?" he says.

"Sorry?" Your hand jerks away from your neck.

He smiles, glancing at your chest, narrowing his eyes. It is an intimate smile, and there is something about it you don't like. This is not a good idea. You glance down at your chest and realize you have unbuttoned the third button. "Oops," you say. Fumbling, you button it up again. And the second one. You look at Duncan MacArthur's face and see it for what it is: old, lined. You know it is not attractive. But you want power over him. You want to feel his rough hands on you. His cologne smells of cognac and cigars.

Images are coming to you unbidden. You see yourself bent forward over his desk, your skirt hiked up, your nylons ripped down. His rigid cock ramming into you from behind. Your white skin quivering with each thrust. And outside the blinds, the hum of the photocopy machine.

You try to concentrate. You look ouside the cubicle, at the fluorescent light and grey dividers. An everyday office. "Yeah," you say. "That's the thing. We're thinking it would have a great deal of popular appeal. Without being too cheap. We were hoping to sort of bridge the gap between the academic and the . . . and the . . ."

"Listen," he says, leaning forward with that funny smile. "Would you like to go out and discuss this over lunch? Or a drink?"

You don't at all like the way he is smiling. You realize you must be very careful here. You concentrate on slowing your breathing. "Actually." You straighten your skirt. "I'm fine to just sit here and talk. If that's okay with you." You clear your throat and sit up straight. "Anyway. What we were thinking is that there is really no kind of public discussion of these, these sorts of . . ."

You talk for long enough that your body goes cold. You are relieved. You continue, businesslike. Duncan MacArthur sits back and listens, nods. You can't believe what you just almost did. When the meeting is over, you leave quickly, eager to get way from the tobacco cologne, that image of his stiff cock under the dark, fine wool. On your way out, you glance through the picture window on the harbour. *Patrice. You bastard. Patrice.*

VII

When you return to your apartment a letter awaits you. It is typed in uneven letters on an old typewriter.

D. –

You know, I don't think, after you come all tied up, against that buzzing cock-ring pressed mercilessly against your clit, with your arms and legs outstretched and trapped so they can't bend, and my body is weighing heavy on you, sweat on my neck, and my cock swollen and about to burst in you – I don't think I will come. I will hold it while you twist and fight against the ropes and moan. And I will pull out and unstrap you and turn you over. And then I will tie you up again: your arms wide, your legs wide apart and pulled tight, your slit open, your buttocks spread, your face in the pillow, biting it with your teeth and clenched. And I will slide into your cunt from behind, while it's still quivering and contracting from coming, fill you with my distended cock, and fuck you slowly, gently, with my chest weighing on your back, my hands under your shoulders and holding you tight to me, sliding in and out with a wet sound, then gradually faster and harder, until I'm fucking you hard, slamming into you with little slaps of my hips against your bum, the vibrating button buzzing against your asshole every time it hits, and I'm panting and grunting. You want to raise your hips, go up on your knees, but you can't; you are flattened against the bed with your legs wide apart. You feel the sweat beginning to slip out of me, and you are saying, "Oh, oh, oh." And I am taking your hair in my teeth, holding your shoulders down with my palms, reaching under you and cupping your breasts, biting your neck, grunting, about to come, "Huh. Huh. Huh." I unbutton the cock ring and release it, let the rapids shoot out, like a water balloon being burst inside you, like hot lead I am shooting out, with a long moan. You feel my cock jerking inside you hysterically. We relax together, panting. And then I roll off you and unstrap you, and you turn to face me and we lie side by side as tight as we can, with our arms wrapping each

other, and my cock slips into you again, you are so wet it's easy, and my
cock is sore and red; I wince a little as it slips into you, and we lie
together, rocking gently, while my cock subsides in you, and we kiss
each other lightly all over the face and neck and shoulders and nipples
and I take your neck in my hands and say over and over again, "I love
you. I love you."
P.

After you masturbate yourself to sleep again, you hate Patrice with a fury.

Back in your city, you are spending a lot of evenings out. You find your-self at karaoke bars with drunken film crews, at black-tie galas with cor-porate fundraisers. You are flirting with 25-year-old cinematographers with ponytails, with 50-year-old executives with blue blazers. You feel reckless.

You go to martini bars after work and talk on your cellphone, feeling unreal. Young lawyers ask you out to dinner and you turn them down; you end up dining alone in hotel bars after receptions. You eat rare steaks, sashimi, couscous with violent chili pastes, tuna tartare, rack of lamb in tarry reductions that sting with rosemary as sharp as pine. You drink blood red wines.

You are sitting at the long marble bar of the Bar Verona one night, swirling the manhattan in your glass and looking at the forearms of the black bartender with the dreadlocks – there is something about bartend-ers' forearms which is, you have to admit, always lovely – and listening to the angular jazz and waiting for the crowd to thicken with tv producers with big black-framed glasses and Mediterranean boys with billowing rayon shirts and girls in tight little strappy summer tops and brown shoulders, when you glimpse a head and shoulders through the other heads and shoulders clustered around the espresso machine that makes you sit up straight and still. For a second it looked like the back of Patrice's head.

And yet it couldn't be Patrice, for this man is wearing a suit and tie, and has his hair slicked back like a Latin lover from a 1950s film. You lose the head from sight for a moment. You realize your heart is beating fast. If it is Patrice, which it couldn't be, but if it is, why didn't he tell you he was back in town? Who is he here with?

You turn back to your manhattan, feeling waves of heat and shiver passing over your body. A man sits at the stool next to yours, but you don't look at him. You try to concentrate on the bartender's forearms.

You sense that the man has turned towards you, is too close and staring at you. So you look up at him.

Patrice smiles at you. It is him, and it is a suit, too; a beautiful navy two-button, and a green tie. His chin is smoothly shaven, which is rare for him. His shirt has cufflinks, his shoes are shiny leather. "Can I buy you a drink?"

You try not to seem too alarmed, or even surprised. "No, thank you."

"How are you?"

You take a gulp from your manhattan. You feel like a cigarette, although you haven't smoked for seven years. You finally say, "Are you on a date?"

He laughs, shakes his head. "I had to come back into town for some business."

"I went past your apartment today. It was all dark."

"I'm not staying there. I have a . . . I'm looking after a house. For a friend."

"Do you dress like that in it?"

He answers this perfectly seriously and sincerely. "Yes I do."

"It must be a nice house."

"Yes it is."

You look him up and down, at the navy suit, the green tie. He looks like a model in a magazine. "Blue and green should never be seen," you say. "My mother used to say."

"Do you think she was right?"

"No. You look lovely. I'm just impressed that you could match them. I've never seen you dressed like this before. I didn't know you had clothes like this."

"There are lots of things about me you don't know."

You are quiet for a minute. "Do you have a secret life?"

"You are my secret life."

You roll your eyes. "Come on."

"All right. Many parts of my life are secret. Would you like to see into one of them?"

Your hand is trembling as you raise the icy long-stemmed glass to your lips. You don't want to betray how desperately you do, indeed, want to answer yes to this question. You say, "I think you should have called me if you were going to be in town."

He puffs air through his lips, quickly and derisively. "Come on, Diana. You're not like that. You're more interesting than that. You know I'm not like that."

"What are you talking about? I would think that calling me would be a totally normal thing to do."

"Precisely."

This silences you for a moment.

The bartender slides a martini towards him. "Thank you." Patrice turns to you. "It may be normal, but it wouldn't be very artistic. Or sensual. You're not normal. And you don't want to be."

"And you know what I want?" you say scornfully.

"Yes."

The way he says this so shortly and casually makes the butterflies rise in your stomach again, it makes you blush and feel a tingling in your groin. "Well," you say more softly. "What do I want?"

"You want someone to be in control. In complete control."

"What kind of control?"

"Sexual control."

The word *sexual* sends another shiver through your abdomen. As slowly as you can, you say, "And what does sexual control involve?"

"The greatest pleasure comes from total vulnerability. When you are totally submissive and helpless, you are in fact an object of pure sexual desire, and you are at your most powerful. You are also at your most arousable."

Blushing, you say, "It sounds scary."

"It is."

You clear your throat. "Damon," you say, "may I have another manhattan, please?"

There is a long silence before Patrice says, "I love the way the bottles glow on that wall."

"Yes. It's lovely."

"And can you see the curve of that woman's breast, through her blouse? There. On your right. The way she is leaning."

"Yes. She's lovely."

"It is," says Patrice, "a perfectly smooth curve."

"Take me to your house," you say quickly.

"I told you, it's not my house. I'm taking care of it."

"Where is it?"

"In Yorkville."

"Of course. Are you there alone?"

"Sometimes."

This sends a fine sliver of pain through your middle. You have never felt the jealousy you feel of Patrice. "Take me there."

"I will give you a time and a date. And when you show up there you will be . . . totally mine. You will be my slave."

The bar seems to swirl around you, orange and chrome. Your heart is beating. "All right."

"Are you willing to do exactly what I say, with no hesitation?"

"Yes. Let's go."

He shakes his head. "The time and place must be of my choosing. I must be in control. And there's one other thing."

"Yes."

"I want you to do the same thing for me. To control me. In return."

You want to kiss his neck, but know he will not let you. "All right," you say, breathless. You feel as if everyone is staring at you, as if you are totally naked in that jazz-prickling bar.

"Wednesday evening, next week, then." He gives you the address: one of those wealthy residential streets north of Yorkville, between Avenue and St. George. He kisses you softly on the forehead and slips away. He does not leave a phone number.

The next week you spend in near constant arousal and fear. As the day approaches you have flutters in your belly the whole time. Does he have another lover? You hardly care. You are going to be with him again.

Is he into pain? That's not what you want. But you don't know what you want. You don't know what to expect. One thing of which you are aware – when you step out of the shower dripping, when you stand in front of the mirror – is that you want to be naked with him, for him to see you naked and admire you.

In the evening, a cool fall evening, you step out of a taxi on a leafy Victorian street. The narrow houses are luxurious, hidden by high hedges and wrought-iron fences, with European cars on the cobblestoned drive-ways, grand pianos through the curtains, lamp-glow through the stained glass windows in the doors. You walk up the path to his house.

The garden smells of wet roses. You have on your little black dress, bare legs, no bra, a lacy black thong. Your hair is washed and clean and brushes your neck; you wear a sharp, dark perfume – Fendi, perhaps, or Halston, or something sweet and heavy, like Coco. You breathe too fast as you ring the bell, which chimes deeply behind the door, as if muffled by velvet.

Patrice comes to the door in an even darker suit – charcoal, with a faint pinstripe, and a silver tie. He has a fine crystal glass filled with amber liquid in his hand; he gives off a distant scent of musk, leather and sea. As you follow him inside – onto thick Oriental rugs – you smile, because black and navy is another combination your mother warned you "didn't match."

He leads you into a living room and your heart almost stops, for there is another woman waiting there, waiting by the mantelpiece. You realize you are hardly surprised, that you knew all along that Patrice would do this to you.

But you are surprised by what she looks like. She is older than you, perhaps forty, even forty-five. She is steely-hard: she has metallic blonde hair pulled back in a severe ponytail, cold grey eyes, noble features. She wears almost no makeup, except a subdued beige-rust lipstick; you realize she is beautiful, or would be if she weren't frowning so disdainfully. She has a perfect figure, too, in her sleek dark suit: she shows much tanned cleavage. Her legs are smooth in black stockings with a seam running up the back; her short skirt clings so tightly to her buttocks that you can see the outline of a garter belt along her thighs. "This is my friend from Italy," says Patrice, "Signora Liscia."

She says nothing, but one eyebrow arches and her perfect mouth twitches, for a second, into a wry half-smile. She too is holding a glowing drink. You would love one; your mouth is parched, but no one offers you one; indeed, no one asks you to sit down and you realize you are not to. So you stand in the centre of the room, on a plush silk rug, in the lamplight, and wait. "The rules are simple," he says. "You must do everything I say immediately, without hesitation. You are my plaything."

He sits with the Italian woman – are you to call her Signora? Or to speak to her at all? – on the sofa, which is covered with a paisley silk shawl.

He crosses his legs – and when she crosses her legs her skirt rides up, you catch a glimpse of tanned thigh and garter and you just know that she wears no underwear. They are both scrutinizing you, looking you up and down. "Turn around," she says in a surprisingly gentle voice, the hint of a foreign accent.

You turn around, slowly.

When you face them again, Patrice says, "Lift your skirt up."

You lift your skirt up, suddenly feeling shy – after all, you are not perfect, you suddenly think, you are small and mousey, you are nobody, and this strange woman seems so elegant and they are both appraising you so coldly. He says, "Remove your panties."

You do so, awkwardly, almost tripping. You hold your skirt up so that they can stare at your black bush, your pink thighs. He says, "Turn around, lift your skirt up." You turn, knowing that they are staring at your round, pink bum.

You turn to face them again, and he says, quietly, "On all fours."

You go down on your hands and knees on the carpet. He says, "Face the other way."

You turn, your bum to them. You flip your skirt up over your hips. He says, "Put your head down, to the floor."

You lower your head and shoulders to the floor so that your bum is in the air, and you feel silly. Their eyes are on your open ass, your crack, your rough hair, and your face is rubbing against the spiky carpet. You want to get up. He says, "Spread your knees wider." You spread your knees apart so that your vagina feels wide open, your asshole even opening a little in the air, your spine curved like a gymnast's. It is as if you are waiting for someone to enter you, and you are frightened that someone or something will, but you are aroused as well; you feel your labia swelling, you feel them growing sticky. You are half embarrassed that they will see the moisture glistening along the slit, seeping out.

Almost to your disappointment, he says, "Thank you. Stand up." You stand up, blushing. He says to the lady, "Undress her." She stands next to you and gently slips off the straps of your dress; it falls to the floor. Her palms briefly brush your breasts. His eyes are on your nipples hardening in the cool room.

He stands. Naked, you follow him into a candle-lit bedroom with a four-poster bed and heavy white sheets. There are pools of beeswax on the floor, under the pewter sconces. The woman has disappeared. You lie back on the sheets, smooth and soft as pyjamas, with your arms stretched above your head. The sheets smell of lilac. Patrice stands over you, fully dressed, holding his drink. You arch your back under his gaze, stare back at his eyes.

VIII

Patrice opens a heavy wooden chest beside the bed, removes a pair of handcuffs. The handcuffs are lined with fur so as not to hurt your tiny wrists. He cuffs your wrists above your head, then attaches the cuffs to the frame of the bed. You writhe, but you are trapped.

Signora Liscia enters: she has changed. She has removed her skirt and top but kept her high heels and stockings; she wears a leather corset with open cups. Her breasts are firm, supported by the corset, her nipples small and brown. You gasp as you see her crotch: it is shaved, and looks harsh, the lips stark. It is like seeing a small girl with breasts, which is troubling. She carries a light, springy whip like a riding crop.

She barely looks at you, but approaches him and removes his jacket. She loosens his tie, bends to unlace his shoes. He is still looking you in the eyes. His shirt is white and crisp. She removes his cufflinks, unbuttons his shirt. His torso emerges, hardened and defined and smooth. She undoes his belt and his trousers fall, revealing a bulging black silk G-string. The head of his cock, like a little rosy bud, is just poking out of the top of the underwear. She strokes it through the silk, her red fingernails like claws, and his cock emerges, full and shiny.

He steps out of the G-string and stands over you. His cock is over your face, and her hand is on his cock. She pulls and strokes; his cock is turning purple, and his breathing has accelerated. You are jealous of her hand on his cock, of her activity; you want to give him pleasure. You are wet now, watching.

She stands tight against him, gripping his thigh between her legs, rubbing her crotch against his thigh. Her hand is in the small of his back or on his buttocks – you can't see – and she is breathing harder too, and whispering something in his ear. They are so close to you that you can smell their bodies. Her bright red fingernails slip up and down his cock as if they will tear it; now she is rubbing so hard he is gasping. His shoulders are shiny with sweat. He groans and contorts his face, his pelvis jerks, and his cock spurts, one, two, three jets over you; the hot droplets land on your face, your neck, your breasts. You close your eyes against the spray, turn

61

your head, spit and sputter. The droplets instantly cool, turn grey and cold and sticky, but you cannot wipe them off, because your arms are bound.

You are sad and jealous, because it seems anticlimactic, for him to come before you do. You wanted him to make love to you. But he only sits for a minute on the chaise longue, breathing more slowly, while the older woman sits at your side, dragging her long fingernails along your flesh, up to your tender breasts. You look at her with fright, at her hard little nipples, her harsh crotch. You can see wetness along her slit, where she was rubbing herself against him. She is looking intensely into your eyes. Her fingers stroke your bush. She is careful not to scratch you with her nails. Now she is running her fingertips along your slit, opening you. She slips one finger inside you, then two. You are so wet your vagina dribbles. With her other hand she pinches your nipple, just slightly too hard, so that you gasp.

Now she has found your clit, is caressing it, rapidly but lightly, with her fingertip. You moan, your hips begin to rock. You feel your genitals swelling, your muscles tensing.

He is standing now, beside you again, watching closely. His cock is stiffening again, looking red and raw.

The woman is pushing your little button more firmly now, rubbing from side to side without mercy, and you begin to make your high little sounds. You are embarrassed and angry; you don't want to come for her. He did not warn you she would be here. You wanted him alone. You want his cock inside you, and he won't touch you. But you can't help it; her finger is too firm.

Just as you feel your back arching and your vagina contracting, she stops. She pulls away.

She reaches into the wooden chest and pulls out a large rubber dildo, bumpy and veiny like a human cock; just bigger than a normal cock but not so big as to be frightening.

You try to relax, breathing very fast, crossing and uncrossing your legs. You want to come now. She spreads sticky lubricant on the cock and onto you – all over your cunt, on your belly, down your crack. Slowly, she pushes the dildo into you. It fills you, stretches you. Then she begins touching your clit again, lightly, maddeningly lightly.

You begin to moan again. Just as she feels you are about to come, she stops. She slides her palm under your bum and gently slips a finger into your anus. With the other hand she slowly pulls the dildo out and pushes it in again. She slips another finger into your anus, and you feel as full as you can be; you feel as open as a sluice with water rushing out.

You look at Patrice. He kneels on the bed beside you, gently lifts your head so you can take his hard cock in your mouth. His cock tastes salty and sticky; it fills your mouth. Now you are really full. You feel about to burst. Her finger is on your clit again; your hips are pumping up and down, his cock against the roof of your mouth, jerking back and forth, your teeth about to clamp on it, you feel the dam about to burst.

And again she stops. She and he pull out of you at the same moment, leaving you stranded and heaving. "Please," you say, your face red, your groin congested. "Please."

They say nothing. The noble lady leaves the room. He sits beside you and strokes your hair. You don't know what to say. She returns with a soft cloth and a bowl of steaming water. Gently, she wipes your mound with the warm water. It makes you want to pee. Then she pours warm almond oil onto it, massages it into your hairy mound. Then reaches into the chest and pulls out a can of shaving foam and a razor. You realize what she is about to do. The razor frightens you. "No," you say. "Please don't. I don't want to be shaved."

Imperturbably, she sprays the cool foam between your legs. You try to remain perfectly still. You feel the razor drag and tug along the top of your mound; it tingles and tickles. She shaves downward in stripes. You feel the cool air on your skin where the hair has been removed. You feel the razor approach your lips, the delicate hood. She is gentle, careful; you feel the razor's path burning, stinging, tingling along your most tender flesh, stopping, then beginning again. It is exquisite. The exposed skin buzzes. When she is right between your thighs, lifting up your legs to get deep between your buttocks, you feel more naked than you have ever been.

When she has shaved you bare, she wipes you off again with the warm cloth, wiping away all the soap. On your burning skin she rubs the cool almond oil; you almost come just at the touch of it.

Now Patrice climbs on the bed, taking the woman's place between your legs. He snaps a studded leather cock ring around his balls and the base of his cock. His cock stands up like a pole and begins to swell even bigger. The head looks distended, hysterical. He is tearing a condom wrapper, unrolling it over his cock. In a deep voice, he says, "Do you want me to make love to you?"

"Yes," you whisper. "Please."

"Do you want me to come inside you?"

"Yes."

"Do you want me to fuck you?" His voice is soft as velvet.

You know that the woman is watching, and you want her to be jealous. "Yes. Now."

"Say it," he whispers.

"I want you to fuck me."

"Say fuck me."

"Fuck me."

He plunges his cock into you, as deep as he can. You curl your legs up around him. He lowers his full weight onto you like a blanket. You bite into his shoulder, taste the salt of sweat. Your fingers dig into his back, his tense buttocks. You grip his hips with your thighs as he rocks back and forth, plunging into you, then withdrawing almost all the way out, then stabbing back. It feels deep. The leather ring rubs against your clit, stiffening it, teasing it. You are wailing now, you are saying, "Yes, fuck me, fuck me." You think you may come just from the friction of the leather against your swollen nub, your smooth hairless skin.

And just as he feels the walls of your vagina gripping him tight as a hand, he stops. He pulls out.

You are covered in sweat, moaning, "No, no, don't stop."

He unlocks the handcuffs, brings your arms down by your side. He rolls you over onto your front. He pulls your hands into the small of your back and cuffs them together again behind you. Now you can't raise your head far off the bed. Signora Liscia looms over you with her whip.

You squeal as the whip falls. It stings in stripes on your buttocks. After four or five strokes you can feel your round buttocks glowing pink, then red. Everything on your body is red, hot, inflamed.

She stops, and he holds onto your hips and hauls your buttocks into the air. Your face is in the pillow, your arms strapped behind you. He spreads your knees. He spears you with his cock again; his thighs slap against yours. Even swollen by the ring, his cock doesn't feel as big as the dildo did. You want him to fill you, you want to envelop him deep inside you, and you want him to come there. With the muscles of your vagina you clench his cock, milking it. You grit your teeth and say, "Fuck me."

With one hand he reaches around and tortures your clit while he fucks you. He rubs it back and forth, up and down, never letting up. Your arms and shoulders are getting sore from their position, your cheek hot against the pillow. His cock plunges in and out. Again you feel your muscles tightening, your vagina contracting, and you feel his pace increasing, the sweat on his palms on your hips, his moans, and you know that he is about to come, that you are about to come together, and you cry out, "Oh, oh, oh."

And again he stops his massage, very suddenly. He pulls his hand back and runs it over your buttocks. He slows the rhythm of his fucking. You feel the cool, sticky lubricant again in your crack. You feel his finger slip inside your tight opening. You feel his cock sliding out, a loss. Then a second finger inside your ass, stretching you. You clench your teeth and wait.

He pulls his fingers out.

The head of his cock is against your asshole, pushing. There is a brief stab of pain as the swollen head slips inside, then that strange feeling as it moves slowly up inside you, filling your darkness. It feels as if it is pushing its way through a dark mass, your denseness, piercing you. Millimetre by millimetre, he slides it inside you.

Then his finger on your clit again, rubbing, stroking, first lightly, then firmly, then hard, crazy as a buzzer.

Your thighs are shaking with tension. His cock is like a steel rod inside you. The wave of your orgasm begins, and this time he doesn't stop: he holds you tight against him, and your body convulses in waves, one, two, three. You hear him gasping, feel the rod inside you jerking as it convulses too, and you come together; you feel it shooting sperm inside its rubber packet deep inside you.

He collapses on top of you and grips you tight against him as you subside.

When you are still, he slowly, gently pulls out his cock. He uncuffs you, rubs your wrists. You lie side by side, facing each other, your hair in each other's hair, your breasts against his chest. He kisses your eyes, your nose, your mouth. For the first time, you kiss on the lips. He plays with your tongue with his. He is stroking your hair. You run your hands over his shoulders, his chest, his buttocks.

The lady had disappeared, but now she re-enters, fully dressed again. She carries a silver tray with two glasses of ice water. She sits on the side of the bed like a nurse, smiling, and hands you the water as if to two small children. You gulp at the water and give her back the empty glasses. Then she covers you with a heavy white cotton duvet that smells of lilac like the sheets. And she leaves, closing the door behind her.

Under the weight of the duvet, in the candlelight, you feel very sleepy. Before your eyes close, you murmur to him, "Next time . . . your turn."

He wakes you before dawn, says you must leave. He too must be gone by morning. You ask him, "Whose house is this? Is it the . . . Signora's house?" but he will not answer. You dress silently. When you walk through the house, you see no trace of his Italian friend; she has already left. Patrice kisses you tenderly at the door and tells you you will not see him for some time. He is going away again.

IX

But you have your life too. You too must leave, travel, enter the limbo land of airports and train stations. It is a land of fatigue and change, rather like a dream.

You are travelling on business. You are in Montreal on a hot summer day. You have had meetings all morning and come out into the heat of a weekday afternoon where all the people are sitting on cafe terraces, laughing; you are surprised, as always, by the easy sensuality of the Montrealers – and jealous, for you are alone and hot in your Chanel suit and don't fit in.

You walk back to your hotel room in old Montreal, in a warren of narrow streets. You climb the stairs up to your stuffy room, throw your briefcase on the bed, throw the window open. Peeling off your jacket, you lean out the window. Across the alley there is a rundown building which could be another hotel, but this one even worse than yours. You can see right into a room one storey down; the window is open.

Two young men are sitting on the bed, talking. They are shirtless in the heat. They are sitting very close to one another and smiling, and talking intensely. You realize that they must be lovers. One of them has coppery skin and long black hair and a smooth torso; the other has shoulder-length blond hair and blond stubble on his face. He too has a sculpted torso.

Absently, you are removing your clothes in the window: you wriggle out of your skirt, rip off your tights, peel off the spandex top that sticks to your armpits. Your bra slips off and your breasts are free. You rub them with relief in the cooling air from the window, watching the window below.

As you watch, the blond reaches his hand up to his lover's face, caresses his cheek. The dark one – the one you are calling the Latin Lover – smiles, kisses the hand, grabs the wrist.

You are interested because, you realize, you are going to see them kiss, and it always excites you to see boys kiss, especially boys as pretty as these.

Their faces lean together and they kiss, looking each other in the eyes. They kiss gently, then with tongues and wet lips.

You sit on the bed to watch them, and your hand wanders between your legs. Your crotch is itchy, has been for a week or so, because the hair is growing out. It is embarrassing to recount, but you have been shaving there all winter, you don't know why, ever since the night in the strange house in Yorkville when Patrice was the Master and the Italian countess, or whoever she was, his torturer.

It is not the kind of thing you normally do, shaving, but you must admit that since then you have been hyper-aware of your senses, of your sex. You have not seen or heard from Patrice for months. You are trying to forget him. Now you are letting the hair grow out in the hopes that this state of constant arousal will diminish somewhat. It doesn't seem to be working.

Your finger wriggles between your labia. You watch as the two pretty boys fall on each other on the bed. Their hair is tangled, they run their hands over each other's muscles. They are giggling and kissing. They tug at each other's jeans, wriggle out, and you see their cocks spring forth, firm and clean. The Latin Lover is not circumcized; the Aryan Dream is. You are amazed that they have not looked up and seen you yet.

You spread your legs, arch your back. Your finger is working inside your cunt, and you are wet. You feel a red blush on your cheeks and breasts as you see the boys lie together, quiet now, holding each other's cock.

You wish you could be there, between them, feel their rough chins on your breast, have the two cocks to yourself, hold one in each small hand, play with the foreskin – as the blond is doing now – and feel the sticky drops form on the tip.

The blond slides his head down the Latin's torso and takes the uncircumcized cock in his mouth. You gasp; you have never seen two boys do this before. You can almost taste the salty cock in your mouth.

The Latin arches his neck and closes his eyes; his cock slides in and out of the blond's mouth.

You have found your clit now, are rubbing with fever.

The bed you are sitting on is an old one, with a wooden headboard and turned wooden posts making a footboard. You stand and straddle the horizontal bar of the footboard. You have one knee on the bed, the other foot on the ground. With one hand you hold onto the bedpost, with the other you massage your tender, jumping, reddened and swollen little button. Your stubbly lips touch the cold, hard wood.

The boys are sucking each other's cocks now, tangled like snakes. Their muscles glitter with sweat.

You slide your sex back and forth along the wooden pole, leaving a glistening smear of wet. You are close now, your nipples are hard and your breath coming fast.

The boys untangle. The Latin Lover lies on his front, his legs spread. The blond is rolling a condom over his erection. He lies on his friend, his cock buried in his buttocks. You are not sure you want to see this, but you are tight now, close, your breathing is faster and the muscles in your belly are knotting up.

The Latin boy tenses as the blond penetrates him from behind. Their heads are close, they are whispering. You wonder what it feels like for them. You want to be there, to have one cock pushing into your vagina, keeping the other at bay by holding it tight in your fist, feeling it pulsate against your palm.

The blond boy's pelvis is pumping now, first slowly, then firmly; he is gasping. You are making high-pitched squeaks; you are about to explode.

There is a sharp rap at your door. And without a pause, the door opens.

With a squeal, you fall onto the bed, grabbing the bedclothes around you. A young chambermaid has walked in, and stops short, seeing you flailing about, naked.

"Oh!" she says, her hand to her mouth, "Excuse me!" But she doesn't move. She stands in the doorway, staring at you.

You have managed to cover yourself up, and you stare back. She is very young, maybe only twenty, and pretty, with dark hair and dark eyes and dark red lips. She wears a starched uniform with a short skirt. She has a faint smile on her lips – not a mocking smile, but a warm one. She moves towards the window, looks out, and sees what you see.

"Oh," she says with interest, and moves to the window to watch.

You are amused by her nonchalance. You get up, wrapping a sheet around you, and stand beside her. You glance at the wet smear on the footboard, where you were rubbing against it, and hope she doesn't notice it. She giggles a little. She says, with a heavy French accent, "You ave the most entertaining view in the otel!"

Which makes you laugh, too. You cast a sideways glance at her, and notice her glossy hair, pinned up in a neat bun, and the little loose curls on the nape of her neck. Which also makes you giggle – you are not sure why, perhaps you are a little giddy. You have a sudden urge to hug her, as you would hug any of your girlfriends.

She turns to you with her warm smile. "We won't tell anyone."

You blush, and without thinking you put a hand on her waist. She arches her eyebrows, but doesn't move. Very slowly, you move closer to her, until you can feel her breath on your face. She smells of laundry soap. You wonder if she can smell the sex from between your legs, on your hands.

You have never kissed a girl on the lips before. All the times you have touched women, been with women in some sexual way – when Patrice took you to the strip club, when you were with the mysterious Italian lady – and you have never kissed one on the lips. That's the real frontier. You wonder if you are going to. She is smiling mysteriously, her head at an angle as if asking you a question. You don't know what the question is.

You bring one hand up to cup her breast in its crisp cotton uniform. Her breast is as soft as your own.

She leans forward and lightly touches your lips with hers. They are soft, warm. Then she pulls away. "Hexcuse me. I better get back to work."

And she moves to the door. She turns once, and looks at you with big eyes, and rushes out, closing the door behind her.

Your lips are still burning where she kissed you. Between your legs it is still warm and moist. You look down at the open window: the boys have vanished. Their bed is hardly rumpled.

You wonder if any of it really happened.

You let the sheet fall, and collapse naked on the bed. You picture the young Québécois girl's big eyes. You can still feel her breast under your palm. You wonder what would have happened if you had begun to unbutton her dress. You picture her young breasts.

It makes you uneasy, but you can't help imagining touching the rest of her. You imagine your breasts touching, the feel of her hard nipples against yours, the smooth skin of her neck.

You touch yourself again. Your finger slips easily into the wet, between the slippery fold, finds the bursting point.

Your mind is flashing, pictures you haven't allowed yourself before. Her white cotton underwear. The feel of her buttock under your palm. The warmth between her legs. You imagine touching her hairy lips, feeling the wetness, and her humming sounds.

You imagine your bellies together, hot and smooth.

The pleasure is spreading along your thighs, into your middle. You don't know it, but you are yelping. Your neck is arched, your legs spread. You wonder if anyone is watching you from another window in the other hotel – you don't care.

You are alone with yourself now, just clinging to the pressure behind your clit, in all your muscles, pushing it as if to push it over a cliff, and it does – you burst, you wail, the sweat slides from your pores. It comes in waves, snaking along your spine, your arms, convulsing your toes. You think it will never end.

It leaves you panting, on your side, your knees up by your chin, on the bed. Your breathing slows, but your face is buzzing. The room is quiet.

From the open window you hear the hiss of traffic, the rumble of a truck, car horns, the odd Québécois shout; the sound of a Montreal afternoon.

X

You begin to think about getting a boyfriend.

Your friends seem to think it's a good idea. Although your friends' advice is rather confusing: they are convinced that you have to have a boyfriend, that you will not be happy until you do, regardless of whether you seem to be happy now, as you are, indeed apparently happier than they are. They spend their time alternating between telling you how important it is for you to have a partner and complaining about theirs. Their husbands are endlessly sinning: they forget Valentine's day, they cancel holidays. Most important, all husbands seem to lose interest in sex. Your girlfriends need little more than a first cigarette and a preliminary glass of wine to begin lamenting their passive, silent men, their evenings of silent television watching and baby feeding, their snore-filled beds. Then they look at you soulfully and express their fervent wish that you find someone, too.

Since you are having more sex than any of them are, you wonder why it is so important to have a boyfriend.

It is true that you think about Patrice, often, every day, in fact, and with a sudden ache that is like love. But you know that it isn't. You know that it is in fact his insistent hands that you miss, his aggressive thrusting. The way his scent and his elusiveness make your body convulse like petals opening, tremble, run with liquid sex like a subterranean waterfall. It is the sex that you miss, the sex and the danger; the romance of his sudden slicing appearances in your life, the door that he thrusts open on those underwater streams, and just as suddenly slams shut. You know that Patrice would not make a good boyfriend.

In fact, you have given up on Patrice. He has not contacted you for some months, anyway. And you know that there is a yearning in your life; you are not sure what it is for, exactly – it is possibly just a yearning for more sex – but you decide to try to fill it with a boyfriend. You decide to give it a try, anyway. A nice guy, this time.

It is not as if there is a shortage of possibilities. Your girlfriends are delighted, so delighted in setting up your dates that sometimes it seems to you their glee verges on hysteria. This is not encouraging.

The dates themselves seem more like job interviews.

There is the young founder of a small but rapidly expanding software company (check shirt, khaki trousers, firm handshake). There is a director of television commercials (long hair, leather jacket, cellphone). There is a producer of Web-based multimedia entertainment (soft black Armani jacket, black linen shirt, suede shoes, designer spectacles like modernist sculpture). And there is a PhD student in philosophy, or history, or the history of philosophy or something like that (black jeans, messy hair, sideburns, baggy synthetic shirt that says "Snug").

The software guy is by far the wealthiest and by far the worst dressed. The sex with him is exciting, in a dumb preppy boy way: his size, his big sunburned shoulders, his fresh laundry smell, his clumsiness, his earnestness, his boring beige apartment. It's all kind of cute. But the most intense pleasure he can imagine for his leisure hours is off-road cycling, or circling a lake in his powerboat. He is excited about an upcoming vacation, which he has elected to spend – voluntarily chosen, out of all the possible crumbling European cities, all the overgrown tropical temples he could have chosen – at a hot springs resort in Colorado, where there is horseback riding and hill climbing. You cannot picture yourself sharing these pleasures for long. You once shock him, at a business awards reception, by whispering to him you are wearing no panties. The look of panic in his eyes decides you against any further dates.

The commercial director takes you to by far the best parties, and has by far the best car, a tiny convertible antique MG in navy blue, the only MG you have ever seen without rust patches. He introduces you to actors and gangly models. Rather too many gangly models for your liking; he has gone out with most of them, it seems. And he has no trouble talking endlessly to them about their backaches and headaches and the merits of various herbal remedies and macrobiotic diets. The sex with him is intense and inventive, and not without pungent smells (smells have become important to you, you realize), but it doesn't always happen; sometimes he is too nervous and irritable and prefers to smoke in bed with the TV remote in his hand. This is perhaps due to the role cocaine plays in his life; cocaine is an endless source of conversation, boastful reminiscences, excited cellphone dealings, midnight drives. You do not find cocaine so interesting as to accord it such a role in your life. Besides, he owns a pair of cowboy boots. You have managed to dissuade him from actually wearing them in your presence, but his mere ownership of them, their very existence, is dissatisfying enough.

The multimedia producer, who comes next, is the most intelligent so far. But it is these dates which seem most like a job interview. He is smooth, sleek, slim, sallow. His hair and skin are dark, he speaks softly, with a faint smile playing about his lips. He is very handsome, if tired looking. He too has a cellphone, but he (unlike the commercial director) politely turns it off for your dates, slipping the solid black lozenge carefully into the pocket of his black cashmere overcoat, where it sits submissively waiting, in silence as black as his hair and his suede shoes. He fixes his eyes on yours and studies them as he questions you, asking you if you have seen a bleak Danish film, an exhibition of advertising posters. He reads Don DeLillo; he knows who Kasimir Malevich is. He also knows which television shows have the highest ratings, which restaurants are the newest in New York. Conversations with him sometimes seem like a test.

You have the highest expectations of him. You sense that someone so intelligent will be very open-minded in bed. So you do not rush the first encounter. Mindful of the no-panties disaster with the software executive, you are restrained on your dates, no funny business – although you do not refrain from sexy clothes, lycra tops that cling to you like soapy film, stretchy velvet dresses with buttons that you can open to your navel. You lean towards him in candlelit restaurants, smiling, aware of his eyes flicking to your bare shoulder, the visible strap of your blue lacy bra, the scalloped tops of the cups surfacing as the front of your dress billows forward. He is very cool about all this. You are impressed.

But when the first encounter finally happens – in his open-concept loft with its halogen lighting and its industrial kitchen – he seems nervous. He keeps looking at his watch, for there is an important phone call he has to make to Tokyo as soon as it is dawn there. You are so bored with waiting for him to make a move that you have practically forced him into it, unbuttoned your velvet dress so low it is slipping off, standing so close to him as he pours your wine that he could almost penetrate you without shifting his position, and still you had to put your hand on the back of his neatly shaven neck to bring his lips onto yours. And then you sit on the leather sofa kissing and groping for what seems like an hour and a half and he still doesn't have his shirt off and you're wondering what is going on inside his pants.

74

He finally leads you up the spiral steel stairs to the exposed catwalk thing that serves as his bed platform, which you find rather dizzying, and your clothes come off, and then you manage to get his clothes off and you find that he is still limp, which makes you instantly depressed, as it reminds you of the commercial director. You kiss and clutch and stroke for another few minutes until he finally sighs and sits up and says in his soft voice, "I'm sorry. I've been working awfully hard lately. I guess I'm kind of . . . kind of stressed out."

"That's all right."

"I think I'm worried about my phone call."

"You go and make your phone call."

"I think I will." He kisses you quickly, and reaches for his clothes. And that is the end of him.

You don't have any great expectations of the PhD student. He has a funny name: Jones, Jones as a first name. You find it difficult to call him Jones, even though that's his name; you feel as if you should be some kind of Marine buddy in combat to call someone Jones. And he seems kind of geeky, the kind of guy who knows a lot about horror movies and makes endless lists of his favourites. You don't know this; you're just guessing. He's the kind of guy you want to shake up, to get out into the world. To shock.

You go to a rather beery bar with mismatched diner furniture and candles stuck in Jagermeister bottles, where he promptly orders a pitcher of beer, which you take as a surprising sign of a sensible nature. You clink your pint glasses too energetically and splash foam and both laugh. His laugh is whole and natural. He is unshaven too, but his stubble is blond and sparse; it looks as if it would not be scratchy but fluffy. He wears two hoop earrings and worn military boots. His legs are long and awkward; he arrays them on either side of the little table with the grace of a man wearing skis on asphalt. He seems embarrassed by them. He folds his arms across his chest and looks at you and says, "So."

"So."

"So Denise tells me you're really into sex."

You choke on your beer, spit and cough. "Jesus Christ." He said this nonchalantly, without challenge. But it is not the kind of thing you expect someone to say. "Well," you say, wheezing, "that's not the kind of thing . . .

75

that's not the kind of thing I hope . . . that's not the kind of thing I expect Denise to go around saying."

He shrugs. "I think she meant it as a compliment."

You laugh. "Sure. Whatever."

He smiles.

"Denise should *not* go around saying that."

There is a silence. He drains half his pint of beer. You wonder exactly how tall he is. Six four? *Over* six four? It seems possible from this angle.

He says, "Well?"

"Well, yes. I guess I am. Isn't everybody?"

"I don't know. I never have been."

"No? Why not?"

"I don't know. Never had the opportunity, I guess."

Well, you think, *this is a great fucking start*. But you don't say that. You don't even really feel it, you just think you should think it: in fact, something in you has just relaxed. You say, "That's charming."

"Thank you."

"No, I mean it. I'm glad you told me. So what . . . what do you do instead?"

"Well, for the past few years I've really been into my work. My thesis."

"And, remind me, what is –"

"It's history," he says shortly. "History of philosophy, so it's mostly philosophy. But it's in the department of history."

"And what's your –"

"Jansenism. Reformist Catholic religious movement. France, seventeenth century. Pascal, famous adherent." He says this so rapidly you can tell he is sick of explaining it.

You say, "I guess the Jansenists weren't much into sex, is that it?"

"They certainly weren't. They weren't into much but prayer and repentance. They thought they were all going to hell. That most of them were, anyway. But that has nothing to do with me, you know with my own . . ."

"Why did they think they were going to hell?"

"Do you really want to know?"

You take a long pull of beer. It tastes golden, like metallic flowers. You feel its warmth spreading through your belly, and sit back in your chair. You stretch your legs out so that they touch his beside the table. The bar is dim and warm, its noise fuzzy and low. "Yes, I do. Tell me what you know about and I'll tell you what . . . whatever you want to know."

He laughs his deep, open laugh once again. "All right. Cheers. Do you like this song? I like this song."

"Yes I do."

He growls, "*Check it out now, the funk soul brother.* Are you sure you want to know about the Jansenists?"

"I want to know about you. So yes, I want to know about the Jansenists. And it might be something useful to know at cocktail parties."

He makes a noise like a bark. "No, it probably won't come up at cocktail parties. It's not the kind of thing that does."

You realize his bark was a laugh. You think suddenly of the multimedia entertainment producer, and how something like Jansenism was indeed quite likely to come into his conversation. You say, "I have to meet with a lot of writers lately. It's the kind of thing that comes up."

"*Right about now, the funk soul brother.* Okay. Let's start with the Reformation."

He tells you about Calvin and Luther and the Catholic reaction, the pure Jesuits, the extremist Jansenists, the monastery they lived in called Port Royal, their severe faith. He tells you about Pascal, the mad mathematician, and Racine, the playwright who wrote tearful tragedies that always end in death, death all around, a pile of bodies backstage.

You say, "It sounds as if they were sexually repressed."

"No, oh no, they weren't repressed at all, it was an extremely sensual culture. Racine, hell, Racine is a, Racine is the most passionate playwright you've ever read, it's all about desire and passion and beauty and the senses, but it's all deadly, there's death behind everything, death and God." He is speaking rapidly now, gesturing with his glass, splashing beer. "And the music, God, the music is so sensual. Have you ever heard Sainte-Colombe? It's viola music, viola da gamba, like a precursor to the cello, it's so deep and rich and, I don't know, melancholy, it's . . ."

"Sexy."

"Yes, I guess, I guess it is sexy."

You lean forward, circle his forearms with your little hands.

As you do this you realize that you would not have done this a year ago, or even six months ago. There is Patrice behind this action – Patrice behind you, now, almost literally, as if he is standing in the shadows of the bar or sitting at a table across the room, appraising you, with his fingertips together. Approving of you.

When you were with Patrice, it was you who wanted to be taken, led, frightened, passive. You wanted the excitement of Patrice's mystery, the excitement of his control, of having no responsibility. And now you are taking control, shocking this gentle man Jones with your aggression, and you have not changed, really: you want to provoke the same passions, the same impromptus, the same electric buzzes of surprise and apprehension, that you will share with someone, and you want to share it with Jones – why Jones, you don't know, perhaps because you sense a sensitivity in him, perhaps because he makes you feel more powerful in some way than he is – and it doesn't matter, it really doesn't matter if it is you who is taking the lead or he. And if it must be you who takes the lead, who creates the suprises, you will do it well, for Patrice has taught you well. There is little difference in leading or being led. Patrice has brought out the fearless in you, and now you will share that fearlessness.

So you stroke the bare skin on Jones's long forearms. You take a breath and say, as deeply as you can, "In other words, all this puritanical religion, or intense study of it, in your case, might be an indication of deep, turbulent reserves of . . . ."

"Of what?"

"Of, I don't know. Of turbulence."

"Perhaps." He is very serious, looking down at your fingers stroking his arms, frowning.

You say, "I want you to touch my legs."

He pauses, stares into his beer. He is considering. Under the table, you stretch your legs out – your legs are bare, under a thin summer skirt – and rub against his long, scratchy corduroy legs. You hike your skirt up an inch.

Sighing as if in resignation, he leans forward, swings his hands under the table. His long fingers find your bare knee. Your feel their calluses sliding over your skin. He is staring you in the eyes. His face is flushed. You part your knees a little. His hand runs lightly up your thigh, dipping down between them, caressing the inside of your thigh. His touch is exquisitely light; not hesitant, but gentle.

You close your eyes, sigh.

You reach your hands under the table and grip his bony knee. You feel his breath on your face; your faces are almost touching. You open your eyes and stare into his. He blinks his long lashes. You glide your hand up his thigh, into his crotch. You feel the bulge, a hard shaft. You trace it gently with your fingers until you find the head, a swollen knob like a steel handle. You close your fist around it. He catches his breath.

"Jones," you say, "this is going to be just fine."

He says in a soft, growling voice, "As long as you tell me what to do."

"I will." You release him, lean back. "We can teach each other."

"Teach me something now."

"All right." You look around the crowded bar, at the white girls with dreadlocks and eyebrow rings, at the flappy-pants DJ slapping another guy's hand, at all the drunk sexy young people. You stand up, pick up your little shoulder bag. "I'll be right back."

You stride to the stairs down to the basement washroom, knowing he is watching your skirt shimmer and float as your hips swing, the backs of your bare legs.

In the dankness of the toilet stall, you slip off your dress, your bra, your panties. For a dizzying second you stand there, totally naked, except for your chunky black boots, as girls swear and giggle at the sinks. Then you pull the summer dress back on. You stuff the bra and the panties into your bag, sling it over your shoulder, and walk back up the stairs.

As you squeeze through the crowd, you are sharply aware that you are naked under your dress. Your little breasts sway, the thin fabric brushing against them. Nobody is looking at you.

"Well?" says Jones as you sit down.

You hand him your shoulder bag, trailing its tentacle of bra strap. The bag is open; he can see the crumpled anemone of white lace and silk within, the panties puffing out gusset-upward, a tender stain on display. He stares at it a moment, then extends his long fingers to pick delicately at the trailing strap, as if afraid of burning himself. He looks like a cat poking at an unknown substance, ready to recoil.

"Take out the panties," you say. You cross and uncross your legs. Your face is hot; you feel naked in public. Still no one can tell.

He pulls out the faintly soiled white silk panties, balls them immediately in his fist. He holds them for a minute on his lap, staring down. He

79

seems about to bring them to his face, which you actually hope he won't do. Then he stuffs your panties in his pocket.

You both lean forward simultaneously and he reaches under the table for your knees. You part them under the table as his rough hands roam upwards, gently stroking the insides of your thighs.

You hike your skirt up another inch. Anyone bending over – to pick up a dropped napkin, say, or to tie a bootlace – would find his face at eye level with your bare thighs, your furry bush, your lips gleaming in the shadow under the little cocktail table.

You are breathing fast. So is Jones: his face is flushed, his lips slightly parted. You lock your eyes with his. His hand has reached your groin; his fingertips lightly brush your fur, your lips. You quiver. You feel the lips opening wetly, of their own accord.

You glance around: a flat-topped nineteen-year-old at the bar is watching you closely, a faint smile on his freckled face.

You close your knees, reach down and gently remove Jones's hand. "Okay," you whisper, "this is getting dangerous."

"I thought that was the point."

You laugh. "Very true." You pull your skirt down, stand up, take his hand. "Come on."

You lead him out through a side door into an alley. The door closes behind you with an irrevocable thunk. The air is hot and still. There are garbage bags in piles, and their faintly sweet perfume. You lean against a brick wall, pulling him against you. You shove his hands against your breasts. You lift one knee so your thigh clutches him. You are sucking his warm lips, grasping his buttocks in your palms. Your tongues are embracing; you rub the thick of them together, the thick rasping surfaces of tongue flat together, as if you were both licking ice cream. A drop of saliva drips down your chin; you don't know who it belongs to. You hear the engines of passing cars, the laughter of couples passing on the sidewalk. He has your skirt hiked up, his hands kneading your naked buttocks.

You feel his shaft pressing against your belly. You rip open his belt buckle, unbutton his jeans. You plunge your hands down the front of his pants, grasping his swollen cock. You begin to stroke it with firm fingers, yanking up and down. You are trying to work his trousers down over his ass with your other hand.

He pulls his face away from yours, gasping. His lips are slick. He looks towards the entrance to the alleyway, the sidewalk. People are passing without seeing you.

You wrap your hands around the back of his head, try to pull his face back towards yours. "If they see anything," you whisper, "they'll enjoy it."

But he pulls away, yanks his pants back up to his waist. "I'm sorry," he mutters. He is breathing hard. "I'm scared."

"Of what? Of getting caught? That's the –"

"I know. I know. You don't have to explain it to me. I just . . . I just have to go slow for . . . for the beginning."

You smile, kiss him gently. "Okay." You watch him buckle his belt. You smooth down your skirt. "You've done very well already."

XI

And so begins your relationship with Jones.

You take him shopping in luxury department stores, making him wait while you dress in diaphanous dresses. You step into the light of the store with your nipples showing through the dress, and stand and stare at yourself in the three-way mirror while he sits behind you, smiling, and the shopgirls raise their eyebrows and the matrons frown and their husbands, bored and balding, slumped in the leather armchairs, stare, blush and look away.

You eat oysters with Orvieto at outdoor cafes and talk about the Reformation and the Jansenists; Jones tells you about the mathematics of Pascal and the court of Louis XIV.

The court of Louis XIV sounds like a brilliant and awful place to you.

In your apartment in the late afternoons you strip him naked and lower yourself onto his erection, gritting your teeth and grinding down, as if you were drilling him.

You lick his cock with long, slow strokes from bottom to top and down again, you take the whole of his swollen head in your wet mouth for a second and release it again before he spills. You hold his warm balls in your hand, gently, as you lick. You press the taut band of skin under his balls, betwen his balls and his anus, and he gasps and comes faster, shooting seed onto your cheek and neck in silence, puffing and writhing but holding his moans deep inside.

You drape yourself over tabletops and grasp the hard edges as he thrusts into you from behind, hard and fast and silent. You feel his strong hands on your back, holding you firmly to the cold table.

You teach him to lick you all over, slowly, before he comes to your sex, softly nibbling at the inside of your thighs and moving slowly higher, slowly, then turning you over and spreading your legs and licking your ass, just brushing the hair or your vagina with the tip of his tongue as he licks your inner thighs, gently touching your anus with his tongue, making you quiver. Sometimes he lingers there, as his fingers reach under you to brush your clit through its hood, and thrusts the tip of his tongue right into your anus, making you gasp and squirm and shiver as his fingertip strokes your clit.

You teach him to slow down as he licks your sex, to make the circles he makes with his tongue smaller, lighter and slower, to not speed up as your body clenches and your breaths come faster, to wait and wait for it to develop, to spend long minutes – fifteen, twenty, a half-hour – with his head buried in your wetness, dream periods in which time does not seem to pass, with you on the edge of orgasm, as he snuffles and gasps at your crotch, his long arms reaching up to cup your breasts and stroke your nipples. Your eyes are closed and you are far away for what seems like days, passing close to the edge and back again, before you finally erupt with long shudders, and he does not relent, does not change his slow rhythm, pinning your hips down with his hands and continues his insistent, regular, now almost painful circular nuzzling, so that you shudder and shudder again, moaning and shrieking.

On one drowsy afternoon, with rain softening the light, you bathe him in an oily, scented bath, and when he emerges, glistening and hard, you lay him on a towel on your bed and shave the hair from his groin, carefully stroking the razor around his distended cock, moving it carefully from one side to the other as you shave, seeing his childlike flesh emerge. You shave his nipples and his chest and the arrow of hair that runs from his pubes to his navel, rubbing soothing oil into the smooth skin as you finish, so that when he rises he is shining, muscular, hairless as a statue, an eerie child-man, an androgyne who nevertheless pushes his sex into you as hard as a man.

You have fun with Jones but you sometimes miss having someone else in control. You are never out of control with Jones.

You convince him to accompany you to a fetish party at a night club, a dungeon night where there is a strict dress code of leather or latex or lingerie. You dress him in heavy black boots, tight black shorts, a tight black T-shirt. You wear a black PVC catsuit with a zipper down the front that goes right between your legs and up your ass to your tailbone, so that if you were to open it all the way it would allow easy access to all of you, everything. Not that you intend that to happen. But the zipper up the crack of your ass is an erotic concept.

And you match it with stiletto heels. The catsuit sucks to you, squeaks as you walk; it covers you from ankle to wrist to neck in shiny plastic; it gives you total smoothness, firmness, the sheen of a machine. And it is so thin and tight you cannot wear any underwear under it, just your own sweat. You pull the zipper down low to reveal the inner halves of your breasts; you know the nipples are prominent through the vinyl, too. You practice with the heels in front of a mirror for a while before you feel able to walk more than a few feet. You stride around your bedroom – Jones on the bed watching, serious, considering, his penis hard in his shiny black shorts – amazed at how your legs have grown long and taut, your buttocks firm and protruding. Even the discomfort, the stress in your calf muscles, is part of the arousal you feel, seeing yourself as a dominatrix. For that is what you look like now, like a walking illustration, a glittering ice-princess with straight black hair and spikes for heels, her feet arched like a dancer's.

The club is almost totally dark, the booming beat deafening. You pay a ludicrous sum to get in, handing your crumpled twenties through the bars of a cage to a malnourished boy with a pale chest and pierced nipples and jagged black tattoos on his shoulders. Around his arms are leather bonds studded with spikes and D-rings; his eyes are underscored with black. You cannot see what he is wearing beneath the counter; he may be completely naked. You both want and don't want to look down and see what piercings, what metal hardware sprouts from his cock. He crouches there in his cage scowling like a gargoyle. You imagine an enormous muscle-man with a shaved head letting him out at the end of the night, leashing him and leading him away for his unimaginable degradations.

Past the two bouncers at a curtain leading onto the dance floor (yes, they are enormous and they both have shaved heads), you enter the noise and the swirling smoke. All you see, at first, is silhouettes of uncertain gender, whirling: the domes of shaved heads, the dark slivers of ponytails, boots and heels and shoulders. As you walk through the massed crowd to the bar, you distinguish muscular men in leather harnesses, studded jock-straps; lithe boys kissing each other; sleek dominatrixes – looking just like you! – leading gagged mummies around on leashes, making them kneel at their feet. You see women dancing alone in lingerie that makes them look like catalogue models: stockings with lace tops, garter belts, lacy black thongs, push-up bras. Their buttocks quiver in the strobe lights. Leaning against the bar close to you is a woman in a white lab coat and a little nurse's cap with a red cross. As she leans towards her drink her lab coat glints, for it and the nurse's cap are made of vinyl as shiny as your catsuit. Her lab coat is unbuttoned; it parts to reveal a black lace bra and garter belt. Her stockings have a single seam up the back of her legs.

You are aroused, just on seeing these outfits. But you are tense as well: you feel hungry eyes on you, a shift in the crowd of leather-clad men around the bar, like jaws opening to let you enter. Jones sticks close to you, holding your hand or pulling you to him by the waist. You are grateful for his great height; he towers over the witch-vampire bartender. You order beers and find a wall to lean against. You lean back against him, facing the dance floor. He holds you by the waist. Your head is against his wide chest. You watch, both swaying a little to the violent booming.

You watch men in wigs and high heels and miniskirts dancing with sturdy, short-haired women in police uniforms. You watch as a woman in a diaphanous minidress, clearly wearing no underwear, stands up on the bar to the cheers of the leather men, swivelling her hips to the music, and slowly raises her filmy skirt. For a minute you stand directly under her, in her red shadow, staring up her shaved legs at her shaved vagina, her lips looking strangely raw and troubling. The bartender politely but firmly helps her down, and the crowd applauds.

As you watch, Jones is rubbing his hands all over you, grinding his pelvis against your ass. He cups both your breasts with his big palms. You wiggle against him, conscious of the men watching, serious and unsmiling, coolly and professionally watching. You feel Jones's cock hardening in his thin shorts. You reach around and rub his hips, clutch his balls. He flinches and removes your hand. You whisper to him that if you moved away from in front of him, his cock would be clearly visible to all, swollen and shiny in the clingy shorts. He smiles, says, "Don't move away then," and clutches you to him tighter.

You pull away, laughing; he flinches and tries to catch you to hold to him like a shield; he is bending slightly at the waist to hide his protuberance. You slip out of his grasp and catch his hand; you pull him onto the dance floor and spin and spin yourselves to the throbbing.

Clothes are coming off all around you; there is a topless woman laughing next to you, her little breasts jiggling in the smoke. There is a couple embracing and writhing so closely together you are sure he is actually attempting penetration, right there on the dance floor. After a few moments he slips to his knees and sticks his head up her miniskirt. She stands there frozen, her hands clutching the back of his head, her own head tilted back, her eyes closed, her mouth slightly open, her legs apart – he is clutching her buttocks, stabilizing her as his head bobs away at her groin – her knees flexed, her thighs quivering.

You and Jones are separated by a woman dancing closer to you, a woman in a leather bikini and heavy boots. She has long hair she swings around, swatting you with it, enveloping you in a sweet scent. She smiles as she wiggles close to you. You smile back and you dance slowly face to face for a moment, both sets of hips swinging in unison. Slowly, she is edging closer to you. You are aware of Jones behind you, watching. You look over your shoulder at him and smile. He does not smile back. You notice that there is a tall man in a sort of wrestling suit dancing close to him, watching him. You turn back to the woman.

Lightly, she places one gloved hand on your hip. She presses her hips against yours, you oscillate together. Your eyes are locked. You can smell her sweet perfume, see the sweat glistening on her forehead, on her smooth cleavage.

This is fun, but you are nervous. You are aware of Jones behind you; you wonder what advances the wrestler man has made. You turn your head and see Jones hardly dancing at all, looking miserable, staring at you. The man beside him is swaying too close to him, trying to make eye contact.

You feel sorry for Jones. This is perhaps too advanced for him. Gently, you remove your partner's hand from your hip. You smile at her, shrug your shoulders, and dance away. She smiles too, and shrugs.

You pull back to Jones, wrap your arms around him. You both move away from the man who was trying to seduce Jones.

"*Sehnsucht*", scream the massive speakers. The beat is like mechanized concrete hammers on steel beams. "*SEHNSUCHT.*"

Jones gestures to the bar, rolling his eyes. You push through the crowd and grasp the bar, both breathing hard. You smile at each other's sweating faces, rub arms. Jones makes signs for two beers; the noise is far too loud to yell an instruction at the metal-bound bartender. You clasp your wet beers to your chests and turn to watch the dance floor again. Again, the leather men at the bar close around you to appraise you, to run their eyes up and down your sleek shiny surfaces like cold tongues. You cling to Jones.

As you peer through the smoky dancing figures, you are aware of a group of people gathering in an open space beyond some pillars. You cannot see clearly. They appear to be circling around some kind of wooden horse. A tall, studded dominatrix is pacing in the centre, practicing with a long whip. A young woman in black velvet lingerie is led out by two masked women with bare breasts. The girl, like the dominatrix, has long raven hair and creamy pale skin. But where the mistress's lips are dark blood red, the victim's are pale, her eyes not so violently outlined in black. She is blurred. And her hands are tied behind her back.

The two masked women stand on either side of her, holding her firmly for the dominatrix to inspect. The dominatrix stands before her prey, gently passing the tail of the whip over the girl's quivering flesh. The dominatrix is taller, with her steep heels. She stalks around her victim, caressing her with rubber-gloved hands, occasionally flicking at her thighs with the long whip.

You are gripped by this scene, afraid and stimulated. You grab Jones's hand and drag him closer. You stand in the circle of dark people gathered hungrily around this scene in the shadows, watching.

The mistress's assistants clip the girl's bound hands to a standing frame, and step back. There is a spotlight on the girl's white skin now, her chest rising and falling quickly with her breath. The dominatrix is touching her more roughly now, kneading her breasts through the black velvet bra, planting her leg firmly between the girl's thighs to part them, pushing against the black velvet crotch with her shiny waterproof knee. The girl's eyes are closed, her mouth open. The crowd draws in a little more tightly. You notice the leather men from the bar are in the front row of the circle, their arms tightly crossed, their mouths set. They wear black jockstraps or studded G-strings or black boxer briefs; you can see the proud bulges beginning in several of them.

The tall dominatrix tosses her cascade of black hair, hair so black it can only be artificially so, so shiny and blue-black in the weird light that it boasts of its own unnaturalness, like her toxic rubber suit, her radioactive-red lips. She is all technology, the master of the pale and human and vulnerable body lashed to a post before her. This is the game they are playing: the girl is organic body; the mistress is artifice, machine.

With one flick of her wrist she has parted the girl's black velvet bra in the centre; it falls away to reveal white little breasts, tiny pink nipples. The girl flinches.

The dominatrix caresses the upturned breasts, pulls down the black velvet panties to mid-thigh, exposing the girl's trimmed triangle of hair, surprisingly light brown, not a dyed black as you would have expected. You shiver; it makes her even more human.

The dominatrix stands back, smiling cruelly at the surrounding crowd, as if inviting them to admire her handiwork, the girl's vulnerability. The girl's eyes are still closed, but she is quivering; you can tell that being so helplessly on display excites her. The dominatrix kneels to pull the panties off the girl entirely, then throws them into the crowd. She steps back, curls a finger at one of the muscular men – a young one, with black boots and shorts and cropped blond hair. He steps forward, and bows to the mistress. She makes him kneel at her feet, then turns him towards the bound girl. On his knees, he inches close to the girl, then plants his face in her crotch. He reaches up and grabs her hips, and starts nuzzling her groin, her belly, the tops of her thighs. A ripple goes through the girl's body; she plants her feet slightly wider apart and turns her head up to the spotlight. You cannot hear her in the noise, but you know she is moaning.

You cling tighter around Jones's waist. He wraps his long arm around your shoulders, looming over you.

The kneeling boy is licking the bound girl's sex now, openly; you wish you could get closer to see what his tongue is doing. The girl's body tenses; she pushes herself up onto her toes.

The dominatrix steps in, taps the boy on the shoulder, disengages him. Next she invites two men with moustaches together; one stands behind the girl and caresses her breasts with leather-gloved hands; the other kneels in front and tongues her sex.

Each time the girl begins to approach climax, the dominatrix steps in, pulling the men off her, sending them back into the crowd with hard bulges in their pouches.

One man stands against the girl, rubbing his body against her, clutching her buttocks. In the harsh light you can see his face glowing red, his eyes closed in concentration. The dominatrix pulls him off before he comes in his pants.

Then she unclasps the girl, leads her over to the horse or bench that sits in the shadows between two pillars. The spotlight follows them. The bench is on a platform, leather-upholstered, with cuffs at each end for ankles and wrists. The girl steps onto the platform, bends over the horse. Her wrists and ankles are clipped to the base. Her head hangs down over one end. Her bare ass sticks up in the circle of light, whitely.

The dominatrix runs her long black fingertip up the backs of the girl's thighs. Then she reaches in between the thighs, strokes the hairy lips of the girl's sex, parts them. She is standing beside this upturned ass, parting the girl's labia for all to see. She slips two fingers into the darkness between the girl's thighs. The girl writhes. She pulls out her fingers and holds them up in the white spotlight, glistening.

You shiver: you can hardly bear to see this vulnerability, for you know what it feels like: you remember the dim house in Yorkville, that elegant woman's hard fingers being so merciless on you. But the men crowding in are not beautiful, they are not sophisticated; they are just men.

The men are moving closer now, jostling each other as they circle. You have to stand on your toes to see what happens next.

The dominatrix invites spectators to step up and abuse the bound girl, the perfect spherical ass upturned to the spotlight. The music has gone quieter now, moody and throbbing, with a low and indecipherable chanting of words. You can make out the girl's whimpers and moans as people take their turns licking her shoulderblades, thrusting their fingers into her sex, licking her asshole.

You are disgusted, watching, as you see the loser men take their turns, guys in moustaches and pale green thongs between their limp buttocks, guys who don't understand that the perfection of the aesthetic is essential to the eroticism of this scene, guys who wouldn't get to touch a woman any other way. They line up like hungry dogs.

And yet you are excited. A part of you wants the man in the moustache and hairy chest to be bending over you, splitting you with his huge bulging cock, nailing you to the leather bench. If you weren't tied up, you think, there would be no way to allow yourself to have sex with this man. If you are helpless, you can have sex with anyone, and it's not your fault. It's not your fault you are so tasteless you want this hairy man with his tacky G-string and distended, embarrassing cock to desire you, to be so excited his face is gaunt with yearning as he rubs against

89

your pristine, vulnerable buttocks. If you are tied up, it's not your choice.

The girl's ass and thighs are wet now and shining. A man has two fingers in her anus. She writhes, shivers and moans. The dominatrix stands at her head, caressing her long hair, bending low to murmur in her ear. The dominatrix has become her protector. You turn away, dragging Jones with you. You feel shivery, even though you are so hot you are sweating.

You lean against the bar, suck on your beer and shout in his ear, "That was gross."

He nods, an undecipherable expression on his face. He strokes your shoulders, kisses your forehead. Your crotch is wet, uncomfortable in the sealed catsuit. Your body feels alive with sweat, running with liquids. Without thinking about it, you tug at the zipper between your breasts, inching it lower, feeling the PVC loosen slightly. A drop slides between your breasts. You look down at its shining trail.

When you look up, Jones has moved a few feet away from you. Your heart flutters with a momentary panic as you see him talking to a tall young woman with a long brown ponytail and bangs. She wears a leather miniskirt and leather bra, and military boots like a punk. You suddenly fear that Jones will slide noiselessly away into the roaring darkness with this girl and you will be left here alone.

Then you notice that the girl is with someone else, indeed is holding the hand of a muscular grey-haired man behind her, in momentary darkness. You look questioningly at Jones. At that moment all three of them turn to look at you, and Jones holds his hand towards you, palm upward, as if presenting you. The couple looks you up and down, their eyes narrowing. Through the smoke the three of them come towards you.

XII

Jones leads you to a dark corner. The couple follows. He leans against the
wall and turns you so your back is against his chest. He locks his hands
through your arms, pinning you. You can feel his cock hardening again
against your buttocks. You notice briefly, as if looking on from afar, that
your legs are aching from standing so long in the high heels. The young
woman and the grey haired man – he has a bare chest, cut like a relief map,
smooth dunes of muscles – stand in front of you, unsmiling. She stands
close to you, so close her breasts brush against yours, and you can smell her
sweet perfume.

She rubs her belly against yours. You turn your head away but still she
brushes your lips with hers. She cups both your breasts with her small
hands, and you sigh. Jones is holding you firmly against him. You are
amazed at this turn in Jones: how did he suddenly grow so aggressive?
Sometimes he gets this way after his fourth beer; a fearless Jones, a take-
the-lead Jones, a Jones sometimes even slightly like . . . you cannot think
for long, because the girl's breath is on your neck, her knee between your
thighs, pressing. Jones is breathing on the other side of your neck, nuzzling you, kissing you beneath the ear. You know that he is trying to
remind you that he is there, massively there behind you, controlling the
action.

You let your muscles relax a little as the girl tugs down your zipper.
The shiny fabric parts, your breasts push out into the air. She circles your
bare nipples with her fingertips, making them hard.

The man is standing at your side now, his firm thigh hard against
yours. His hands pass over your body now, too. He bends and kisses your
breasts, flicks at your nipples with his tongue; for one giddy second you
feel each breast being sucked on by a different person, the man and the
girl's heads side by side like siblings at your breasts. You writhe and try to
pull away; Jones holds you firm.

A hand is tugging ever downward on your zipper; you feel your belly
being opened up, then the top of your pubic hair emerges. You gasp, looking around in shame – and it's true, a small crowd has gathered, men and

women alike, to watch your exposure by these strangers. You feel the man's hand delve into your crotch, cup your mound. Gently, he strokes your lips with his fingers. Jones lets go of one of your arms. You keep it tightly to your side, wondering what he is going to do with his free hand. He reaches around from between your legs and tugs the zipper all the way around, so that it opens up to the top of your buttocks, splitting you right open, a strip of you naked right down your centre. From behind, he cups your bare buttock with a strong hand.

The grey-haired man is pushing against you now, his fingers delving into your wet folds, then sliding up to gently rub your clit. Your body is tensing; you feel the blood rushing, the excitement beginning. You throw your head back. You are completely helpless now; you must let everything happen.

Jones's hand slips between your buttocks. His finger seeks your asshole. The girl is licking your breasts. The man falls to his knees and pushes his mouth into your crotch.

Your eyes are closed, as you feel his tongue seeking out your clit, flicking at your parted lips. You part your thighs further to allow him access. Jones's finger slides up your ass. You feel grasped, sucked, penetrated from all sides; you squeal and shudder as you feel an orgasm coming on.

Jones feels your contractions, and suddenly pulls his finger out. He taps the man on the shoulder, pushes the girl away. They stand back, smiling, wiping the wetness from their mouths. You moan, open your eyes, gasp in frustration. Their faces are flushed, giddy. You feel abandoned, wet and open.

Jones releases his grip on your arms, turns you to face him. He kisses you deeply on the mouth; you fall limp against him. He pulls the zipper through your legs, up your front, sealing your heat and liquid inside again.

And then he leads you away again, away from your team of brief lovers, towards a dark archway.

You enter a back room, so dark you cannot tell if the forms you brush against are bodies or furniture. The club's music is muffled inside; the air is tense and still, as if the shadows are holding their breath with desire. Jones lifts you onto a padded bench with your back against a pillowed wall. The room is like a black womb. He spreads your legs and pushes his hips aginst yours. He kisses you deeply, excited and rough. He is again unzipping your costume, working your breasts free.

92

You blink in the darkness, your hands around his shoulders, trying to see. There are shapes moving around you, bodies writhing and fumbling on the benches that line the walls. You can hear grunts and moans over the music. Your hand brushes bare flesh, someone else's flesh next to you, a hairy limb.

"What's got into you?" you gasp.

Jones is determinedly freeing you from your catsuit. He says, in a soft voice, "Isn't this what you want from me?"

You are silent, so he continues his rough work. Now he is jerking down his own shorts so that his cock springs free, slaps against your belly. "Wait," you murmur. You don't want to be completely naked in a room of dark shapes, without seeing where you are or who or what surrounds you. "This is crazy."

He is breathing hard, grunting at your ear. He reaches between your legs, guides his shaft into your crotch. You feel the blunt knob straining against your closed vagina, working between the already slick lips. They part to welcome the swollen head, a pleasure so intense and frightening in this darkness that it is abandonment itself.

"Wait," you say, grabbing his hair with both fists and lifting up his head. You jerk your pelvis back, wriggle away from him. "Protection."

This is the first time he has ever tried to penetrate you without a condom on.

He stops, takes your face in his hand. "We don't need protection any more. Don't you trust me?"

You are silent, trying to study his invisible face in the darkness. It is true that you are still on the pill; you have been wearing condoms for other reasons. But now you know all you need to know about Jones, you do trust him. You know he is safe. But the grunting shapes are moving closer in this dark room; there are too many boundaries being crossed all at once.

"Yes," you say. "I do. But not here. When we get home."

In the taxi you are both silent. You lean deep into the seats with your street clothes covering your sodden, smoke-ridden fetish garb. He turns to you and presses his palm against your crotch, through your jeans and through your plastic skin, and rubs firmly, in circles, until you feel your orgasm finally coming, sudden and silent, finally. You open your mouth wide and noiselessly, your face contorted, as you writhe in the back of the cab, coming and coming.

When you have subsided, avoiding the cabbie's curious eyes in the rear-view mirror, you are exhausted. You smile at Jones, and lean your head against the back of the seat as if you could sleep there. You clasp Jones's hand tightly. You look at your hands lying together between you on the cool vinyl. The city lights flash across you in moving bands.

You go back to your apartment. In silence you both strip off your layers of clothes. You brush your teeth side by side in the bathroom, splash your faces with cool water. Your bedroom is pitch black. You enter without switching on the light, and he pushes you onto the unmade bed. The air is close with the smell of unwashed bedclothes and talcum powder. You are not used to feeling his nakedness in total darkness. You trace the outline of his face with your fingertips, grasp his penis with your fist and find it hard and throbbing. He pushes you back in the blackness and lies on top of you.

His anonymity, in the darkness, the secrecy and intimacy of darkness excite you. You spread your legs and he thrusts inside you, hard, and keeps thrusting. He has been containing himself all night and now he feels full of seed, pent up. He raises your legs in the air and pumps and pumps, harder than he has ever fucked you, making short grunts, as you gasp, shocked by his aggressiveness. He is not waiting for you to come again; he wants to come inside you.

You feel his breathing growing rapid and shallow, his penis swelling and jerking inside you, and he pauses. He withdraws a little, waiting.

He is not wearing a condom.

"Yes," you whisper. "Yes. Come inside me."

With a moan of relief or joy, he thrusts again, as deep and hard as he can. He thrusts and thrusts and you feel him bursting, his cock fibrillating, jumping back and forth inside you as it pumps.

He shudders and moans, shudders and moans, and slumps on you with all his weight.

You giggle a little, stroking his hair. After a few seconds he lifts his head to kiss your eyes, your neck, your nipples, your mouth, making little cooing noises.

He rolls off you and, with his arm draped heavy across your chest, begins to breathe deeply.

94

You lie in the darkness, feeling the strange nostalgic sensation of sticky goo dribbling out of you, down the crack of your bum and onto the sheets. You part your legs and touch yourself there, bring the wet fingers up to your mouth to taste it. Salty. It must be ten years since you let someone come inside you without a condom. High school. And yet it still feels familiar.

You are proud of Jones, grateful for him and worried for him. You wonder what you will make him do next. You lie awake in the darkness, exhausted and flattered and a little bit sad.

XIII

You convince Jones to come with you to a meeting of a swingers' club. He is making a great deal of progress: he is not shocked by this idea, but he is upset about going to the suburb where the party will be held, the sheer unbelievability of a bar called Horizons in a strip mall called the Knock-wood Plaza. He is already shocked enough that you want to pay for this thirty-dollar cab ride on highways to nowhere, and then the forty-dollar-per-couple "membership fee"; this is more shocking than your desire to see normal people – which, he reminds you, means overweight people – breathing heavily on you and on each other. To that desire Jones just shrugs and smiles and says, "Sure."

When you alight from the cab on the oil-stained asphalt of the plaza parking lot, you feel buffeted by the slipstreams of the trucks on the over-pass overhead. There are highways all around you. The pink light of neon billboards sparkles on the chrome parts of new minivans, parked in rows. You look up, out towards the great expressway that runs along the lake and see the beacons for Sony and Hyundai flashing in the night sky as if float-ing out at sea.

The cab has already roared away. The two of you stand alone in the parking lot for a moment, listening to the thumping of disco seeping from the black glass facade of the Horizons bar.

"Jesus Christ," says Jones finally, and grabs your hand. Resolutely, he strides to the black glass door.

The bar is dark, jewelled with disco lights, the swirling flakes of a mirrorball. The figures are all dark. The place smells as if the rug has been shampooed in floral cologne. You hand over your cash to the perky blonde receptionists at the welcome table, and they remind you more than necessary that everybody is down to earth here and there is no atti-tude and no pressure and that the object is just to have a good time, and hand you your perky nametags. On yours you write, "Leila". You encour-age Jones to write "Fernando" or "Ramon" or something, but he sticks to Jones. You notice that he writes his magic-marker letters much smaller than yours.

At the bar, he orders his regular beer, but you decide that Leila needs a flashier drink than Diana would order, something a little suburban, something the colour of the flashing lights on the dance floor. You order a zombie, without being sure of what a zombie is (Leila would know), and receive a vase-sized glass of sticky pink punch, topped with an umbrella. "Perfect," you say, as Jones raises his eyebrows. "Cheers."

You find no shortage of new friends. Couples with names like Todd and Kathy and Brad and Krystal and Dave and Donna flock around you, women with frosted hairdos and gelled bangs, burly guys with moustaches and sportshirts and dress trousers you know they call slacks, telling you how welcome you are there and how nervous they were the first time and that there is no pressure and that the idea is just to have fun. "We're all just normal people," they keep saying, "we're just as down to earth as anybody else," and you smile and wish you didn't feel like telling them, *that's the problem.* Some of the men won't look you in the eye; instead they pump Jones's hand and tell him he has the cutest little wife.

To escape more of this friendly banter, you drag Jones onto the dance floor for a number of jaunty top-40 numbers which you have never heard; you find that you quite like some of them, in particular a rap-like ditty with the chorus "*I'm gonna stroke you up.*" It makes you want to spin around so your skirt flies up to air a flash of garter belt and stocking top, which you do, while Jones looks on, dancing with his feet and no other part of his body, and shaking his head, as if to say, "Here we go."

The DJ interrupts the song with his amplified voice to proclaim the first dance competitions, with prizes, prizes, prizes! First, there is a sexiest polka prize!

You and Jones stumble around, stepping on each other, wondering how you can make a polka sexy, but one 45-year-old couple whirls around to great applause, because they manage to make the tall blonde woman's skirt fly up at every whirl, revealing long tanned legs and a little red thong.

"Whoo!" you say to Jones, in surprise. The woman has a mom haircut and looks like your old neighbour in the house you grew up in. "It's Mrs Williamson!" you say.

"My my," says Jones, his eyes fixed on her cleavage.

They win the evening's first prize, a limousine ride with a couple of their choice. The limo is waiting outside as the DJ speaks! And ladies and gentlemen boys and girls, *anything* could happen in that limo!

The crowd whoops as the statuesque mom stalks the crowd with her beaming husband, eying potential partners. They pass by you and Jones and she looks you up and down approvingly, but she moves on. You feel a surprising pang of rejection. You start to scrutinize the other couples for what hidden sex appeal they have.

She selects the only other sexy couple there, a tall young man with a brush cut and a busty blonde in leather pants. They lead them out the door to the waiting limousine to whoops and applause.

You don't particularly want to touch the mom or her paunchy husband, but you are jealous of their success. And you feel rejected.

You watch Jones: he is chatting to a woman in a green dress that makes her look like a bridesmaid. She has long blonde hair and dark roots.

You slide up to him and he introduces you; her name is Janet, and her husband, the freckled guy over there in khakis, is Dave. This must be the third Dave you have met tonight, you think, but you don't say it to Jones, because you are too distracted by how Jones is talking to Janet, how animated he is, all smiles and nods. He is staring at her deep cleavage. She is a little plump, and is wearing one powerful push up bra. The green satin material shines as she tosses her stringy hair. Her breasts are freckled.

"I'm bisexual," she announces, smiling mildly, as if she has just said, *I'm a church volunteer*. She looks at you and says, "Are you?"

"No," you say. Then, "Well. Sure, I mean. Maybe. I'm not sure."

"I understand," says Janet, beaming and nodding.

Dave, who has approached, tells you that you are one sexy woman. Then he says to Jones, "My wife gives excellent head."

You giggle, for the conversational tone has changed, all around you, suddenly, as the music has grown louder and faster.

"What's so funny?" says Dave. "Let's face it, that's what we're here for." He punches Jones's shoulder.

"Sure," says Jones.

"I mean, why pretend? Right? I mean why not be honest about it, right?"

"Exactly."

"What do you do?" you ask Janet. "I mean, for a living."

"I'm in marketing," she says brightly. "And I'm a church volunteer."

"LADIES AND GENTLEMEN BOYS AND GIRLS," says the DJ. His voice has the gravelly texture of the over-amplified, a relief-map of deep

98

troughs and valleys. It is so distorted it is almost incomprehensible, like a piece of avant-garde music, a composition of buzzing overtones. It is because you are thinking this that you miss the rest of the announcement, which is about the next dance competition, a "DARE TO BARE DANCE!"

You and your new friends turn to watch the dance floor, as four couples step up to compete in what appears to be a straightforward striptease, at least for the women. There are cheers and whistles as blouses come off and hips are shaken. Then men seem content to watch their wives giggle and strip. One chunky girl gets down to her bra and panties. The tall woman with the short mom haircut has returned from her limo ride, apparently unrumpled, and she stalks onto the dance floor with her husband and begins lifting up her skirt to flash the red thong, her brown and surprisingly lean thighs.

You glance at Jones; he is watching her wide-eyed, a kid's grin on his face.

Then a rather large woman with a face like a trucker struts onto the floor in her strappy heels and her shiny dress. She flips her long hair and her skirt around so they both rise up and swat her friends, who are all applauding her. You like to watch her, this bold Amazonian woman who would not be attractive anywhere else, but is being told she is sexy here. And she is: her meaty thighs are smooth, her breasts huge and rich. You want, for a brief second, to grab fistfuls of them. They would feel warm.

Quickly, in one movement, she lifts her dress over her head, pulls it off and discards it. You gasp: she is completely naked. And smiling and spinning her long black hair around. "Oh my God," you say.

"AND WE HAVE A WINNER!" bawls the DJ.

"Right on," says Jones, appplauding. "Excellent."

You feel a wave of affection for him, and wrap your arm around his waist. Together you watch the woman dance and jiggle, her untrimmed black bush, her floppy breasts and their long nipples, her sagging belly. You realize you would never had noticed this woman had she not become naked.

Jones pulls you closer to him with his long arm, begins passing his palm lightly over your buttocks in your thin dress. He is tracing the line of your panties. On the dance floor, more legs are being flashed, bras exposed. One of the Daves is down to his happy-face boxer shorts. Two women take their tops off and begin doing the Bump, which makes you strangely giddy. All the people here are white, all the exposed flesh white and vulnerable, a tender parade of appendix scars and stretch marks.

You stand behind Jones, sliding your hands into his front pockets. Slowly, so as not to be too visible, you inch your hands down and inwards, flat against his hips. You feel his back stiffening. You reach around, inside his pocket, until you find his penis, stiffening in your palm. He stands very still and quiet, the two of you watching the dancing, nobody watching you. You feel the swollen knob throbbing in your palm.

The dance ends, the giggling dancers pull their shirts back on, smooth their skirts. The large lady has disappeared, probably because once she has her dress on she is invisible again. You are thrilled at Jones's excitement, longing to have him feel it for you, for you more than for anyone else. You whisper to him, "So. You want to go home with one of these?"

He nods, shyly.

"You want to play sex games in some shag-carpeted rec room with one of these? You want the wood-grain panelling, is that it?"

"The smell of laundry," he murmurs.

"What?"

"The smell of laundry soap and dampness, in a basement rec room. The cool dankness. That's what I want. And Mrs Williamson showing me her boobs."

You giggle. "Okay. You can have it. You can have anything you want." You feel extraordinarily close to Jones in this moment. You squeeze his cock tighter in his pants, press your breasts against his broad back. You say, "We can have any couple we like. You know that, right?"

He nods.

"So who is it? You can choose. The best looking are the blonde in the leather pants and the brush-cut guy. They're the youngest, anyway."

"Where?"

"At the bar. The ones that Mrs Williamson chose for her limo ride."

"Oh yeah." He considers. "But we haven't met them yet."

"We can. I'll go over right now."

He is quiet. "They're maybe too good looking."

"Too good-looking? What's wrong with good looking?"

Jones shrugs. "It's hard to explain. I'd be a little, maybe a little intimidated by them. I would be performing a little. If you feel more attractive then they are then you feel a little . . . I don't know."

You smile. "I do. I know exactly what you mean. You feel more confident. In control."

"I guess."

"Okay." You scan the crowd. Freckled Dave waves and smiles at you. "Then how about Dave and Karen or whatever?"

"I think it's Janet."

"Whatever. The church volunteer."

He pauses. "They're maybe a little safer to start with."

You watch Janet in her green dress. She must be in her early 40s. Her cleavage is just so slightly dry; not exactly wrinkled, not yet, but dry. Dave's thin hair is red, his skin is white and hairless. "What would you think of me being with Dave, though?"

Jones makes a face. "Well, you tell me. If you don't like him. –"

"No no," you say quickly. "It's not about me. I want whoever you want. I think this is about you. And Mrs Williamson."

At that moment you see her, the tall blonde in her 40s – mid-40s, possibly late-40s – with the short blonde haircut and the tanned legs and cleavage, the wrinkled skin at her eyes, her rather brutish but clean-cut husband at her side, a tall guy in dress slacks and a sport shirt and a moustache, hand in hand as they walk through the crowd. They seem to know everybody; they kiss a lot of people and laugh. You can picture her at work, in the insurance office where she works, with her large plastic spectacles, her big white plastic earrings. "There she is," you say.

Jones follows her across the room with his eyes.

"That's who you want, isn't it? You want Mrs Williamson."

Jones nods. "I do. I want her to bring me some Cheezies in the rec room, after school."

You laugh. "Well, you can have her. Come on."

XIV

A few minutes later you are sitting on a sofa with this couple, at a low table in a dim corner of the club. Her name is Anita. Her husband is another Todd. He is smiling and largely silent, but he has dropped his hand almost immediately on your knee, as soon as you sat next to him. He is frightening to you, a little bulky, and you have never, ever in your life so much as kissed anybody with a moustache. You don't think you know anybody with a moustache, anybody socially, other than people you do business with in banks and in . . . well, in banks, mostly. But he does have a clean citrussy smell. You wonder what the moustache would feel like between your legs.

You almost forgot your name was Leila when you met them.

Jones is sitting with Anita. She is chatting and laughing a tinkly laugh and smiling at you and at Jones and her husband equally, swirling the ice in what looks like a rye and ginger. She crosses her long brown legs, dangles her red pumps. She leans towards Jones so her blouse falls away from her tight cleavage. She has her hand on the back of his neck, is stroking lightly with her fingertips. Jones is beaming and blushing and casting quick glances at you. You wink at him. He sees Todd's meaty hand on your knee and his smile drops for a second.

There are a lot of glances going back and forth: between you and Jones, you and Anita, Anita and her husband. A force-field of coded signals buzzes between the four points of the table. You are all trying to ascertain your partners' wishes; it is a hestitant, four-way negotiation that must take place invisibly, in silence.

This part takes longer than you would wish. You must hear about how long they have been swingers and what their children are up to (they are all away, interestingly, with one or other of the ex-husband, the ex-wife), and about how they are just down to earth, normal people like everyone else and they don't like any *pressure*, and *attitude*, either.

You are beginning to yawn when the open negotiations finally take place. You are going to their house. You feel slightly detached, as you float through the red light to the coat-rack, as if you should feel more nervousness than you do. Perhaps it is the string of red zombies with little umbrellas on them that now swirl around your stomach and seep into your bloodstream like drifting silt, slowing you down. They have created a kind of sleepy pink veil over your vision, which is not unpleasant. Jones follows you, his hand in yours, as if you are both unsure of who is leading whom.

Then you are in their wide American car, sinking into the leather seats on the wide overpasses. You drive through the candy-coloured lights of the highway pixelboards, and then through miles of strip-mall and industrial park, until you are on the curving streets of their subdivision, the two-car garages, the pale brick mansons.

There is no one on the street when you get out of the car. The air smells of cut grass.

And they do, in fact, have a basement rec room – a den, they call it – with a bar with a little sink in it and tall stools with Naugahyde seats. You are disappointed that there is no little spinning sign on the bar, something that says "The Bar Is Open" with a little black jockey or something. There is, however, deep pile white carpet throughout the house, which satisfies you.

You sit in the cool basement on deep leather sofas and Todd goes behind the bar and asks if you want another zombie. You can hardly remember what a zombie is now, but the very thought of another one sickens you, so you ask for a Scotch, which seems to surprise him somewhat. You think then that it might be the right moment to tell them that your name isn't Leila. But Anita has put on some soft pop music – some white group doing love-song rap that is as sweet as the zombies lazing in your belly; thank God for the coppery edge of Scotch in your mouth.

She is dancing a little behind the sofa where you and Jones are sitting, putting her hands first on your shoulders, then on his; she rumples his hair, bends down to whisper something in his ear so her dress falls even farther from her breasts. You can see her red lace bra, and it gives you a slight shiver, a quick expanding somewhere in your abdomen.

You take a breath and look away. Todd sits beside you on a leather sofa and puts his hand on your knee again, deliberately, without any apparent pleasure. You turn to him and smile, hoping your eyes aren't too unfocused. He smiles back.

103

"So," Anita calls out. "I think we all have too many clothes on."

You can see Jones gulping, searching your eyes with his.

"Feel free to remove yours, Anita," you say.

"I think I just might," she says, falling into a chair and swinging her red pumps over one arm, flashing a glimpse of red thong she rapidly covers again. "But I don't want to be the only one."

"How about a game?" says Todd, standing and going to a cabinet. He opens the stained pine door and rummages.

"Strip poker!" shouts Anita.

"Don't even have the faintest idea how to play poker," you say, a little sharply, perhaps.

"We'll teach you," says Jones, surprisingly.

"And then I'll lose."

"Well, losing is the idea, after all," says Jones gently.

Todd has pulled out a video camera and a tripod. "How about some performances?"

This piques your interest a little. Performance you can do.

Todd is setting up the tripod, snapping a little cassette into the camera. "Who wants to do a little dance? Ladies?"

You say, "Why not the guys?"

Jones shrugs, blushing. It seems to you that Jones has not stopped blushing all night.

Todd has set up the camera behind your sofa. Anita stands and poses in front of it, in front of you – her hands on her hip, her legs apart – and Jones comes over and sits beside you to watch the show.

She swings her hips, lifts up her skirt to half way up her thigh, then drops it again, giggling. You have to admit, she has a long, toned body.

Jones puts his arm around you, dropping his hand onto your breast. his fingers lightly stroke your nipple through your dress. You reach over and lay your hand, palm down, in Jones's crotch. You hear the hissing of the video camera behind you, the tape slowly sliding around and around.

Anita is pushing the straps of her dress off her shoulders, wiggling out of it. It falls to the floor. She turns slowly around, her arms outstretched, in her red bra and red panties and red pumps. You take in her slightly sagging belly, the faint dimpling around her buttocks. You feel Jones's cock growing under your palm. You exert a little pressure, and it grows even more.

"Anyone have any instructions for the lovely Anita?" says Todd in a throaty voice.

You look up at him. "What do you mean?"

"Well, for example . . . why don't you bend over that chair, honey? So we can see your ass a little."

Anita, still smiling, turns her back to you and bends over a straight-backed chair, sticking her ass in the air and parting her legs. She looks behind her to smile at you. She wiggles her ass in the air.

You cross your legs. You don't know why, but you are starting to get wet too, you have a warm, nervous feeling in your belly. Perhaps it's the knowledge that the two men are becoming aroused, and that you are about to rise and focus their desire on you in the same slutty and shameful way – and it's the vulnerability of Anita's pose, the sheer whoreness of opening your ass and sticking it in the air, the raw invitation to a cock to come inside it . . . you look away for a second, crossing and uncrossing your legs again. Jones's finger is circling your nipple now, making it hard. You wriggle away from him.

"Anything you want to see Anita do, Jones?" says Todd.

"Yow," says Jones. "I guess so. Just about everything."

"Sexy, isn't she?"

You know that Todd is looking down at you as he says this, looking down the front of your dress, watching Jones's hand on your breasts. His eyes on you make you hot. His big body, his quietness, is frightening.

Jones says, in a hesitant voice, "I want you to lie down on the sofa. The sofa opposite."

Anita looks at him, narrows her eyes and licks her lips. Without saying a word, she coils serpentine on the leather sofa. The shiny surface makes a hissing noise as she slides her skin over it. She uncoils, stretches out on it.

"Put your feet on the floor," says Jones softly. "And spread your legs."

There is a suspenseful silence as Anita shifts her body to face you, her legs outstretched towards them, her head slumped against the back of the sofa. She parts her legs.

You feel Jones's cock thick and hard under your palm. His hand cups your breast. You rub his cock slowly, in circles. You shift on the sofa, jumpy; you want to be looked at, too.

"Close your eyes," he says to Anita. "And touch yourself."

She opens her mouth and begins caressing her crotch, lightly, slowly, her red fingernails sliding over her red silk mound. She makes a faint moaning noise and turns her head slightly. Her back stiffens; she begins rubbing a little harder.

"How about dropping your pants, honey?" comes Todd's voice from behind you.

Anita opens her eyes and sighs. Then she closes her legs, sits up. "Uh uh." She stands up. "I'm not shedding any more till someone else does. Fair's fair." She is looking straight at you.

You clear your throat, stand up. "All right," you say. You walk to the centre of the carpet, feeling awkward and thin on your heels. You swing your arms. "But I don't know how to do the dance."

"Just do any kind of dance, love," says Anita, sitting and watching you with her long legs over the arm of her sofa, swinging her red pumps.

You stand between them: Anita on one side, the men and the camera on the other. You look at the camera's little black eye, its flashing red light. "I can't dance. I don't know any kind of dance. You'll have to tell me . . ." You make your voice go softer here. "Tell me what you want." You look Jones in the eye. "Whatever you want me to do."

"All right," says Jones. "How about unbuttoning your dress a little."

"You're next, you know," you say as you unbutton the front of your dress. You stop when you reach your navel.

"Now lift up your skirt."

Slowly, you lift the hem of your skirt until you are showing the lacy tops of your stockings and your black garter belt and panties – panties you are quite confident about, sheer mesh with lace flowers at the top. You know your pubic hair is visible through your panties.

You pause like this, taking in Jones's intense eyes on your crotch, then Todd's, as he looks up from his viewfinder, his eyes wide. His face seems flushed now, too. You turn to show Anita, who licks her lips as she eyes you up and down.

You bend over the chair, wiggling your ass at one sofa, then the other. Then you cuddle up to Anita on the sofa, stroking her long legs, nuzzling her ear, burying your nose in her freckled cleavage. She smells of a rich and heavy perfume, something with vanilla in it. As she tries to kiss you, you sit back, pulling out of her reach. You push your dress off your shoulders

106

and it crumples around your waist. Then you peel back the cups of your bra a little, flashing your nipples at her.

"Whoa," says Jones.

In the background, the camera is humming.

"Okay," you say, "who's next?"

"I think shy Mr Jones is next, don't you?" says Anita.

"Jones is my first name," he says in a hoarse voice.

"I know it is, honey."

"Come and sit with us, my love," you say.

Jones lopes over and sits between you, fully clothed. He kisses you on the forehead, then turns towards Anita. She ruffles his hair, strokes the back of his neck, says, "What shall we do with him?"

He is already reaching for her breasts, the insides of her thighs, trying to kiss her face, her belly, anything he can touch of her. He is breathing heavily already. You pull him back towards you. "Not so fast," you say. "A little show and tell first. Sit back."

He leans back into the sofa. Anita begins to unbutton his shirt. You help her pull it off him. His almost hairless chest, his strong shoulders and flat stomach emerge. He blinks towards Todd, obviously more conscious of the camera on his naked body than of what you and Anita are doing to him. You unbutton his belt, unzip his fly.

Anita reaches her hand inside his trousers and he moans. You slip to the floor to unlace his shoes.

Anita has worked his underwear down and has his cock in her hand, swollen and pink. She is stroking it, up and down. Jones has his hands stretched out along the back of the couch, and is biting his lip, his face congested, looking down in amazement at this woman's hand on his cock.

You pull his socks and trousers off. He slumps downward, stretching out, to enable Anita easier access to his cock.

But she eases off, leaning back herself, as if inviting him to touch her. You sit beside him, on the other side, but you realize he is not looking at you; he is waiting for this signal from Anita to come at her with hands and mouth, he is hungry for it – and you decide to leave him to it.

You slip off the sofa, letting your dress fall to the floor. You kick it off your feet and walk to the other sofa, where Todd stands with his camera, and sit in front of him. You watch Jones and Anita – *Mrs Williamson*, you think – begin to kiss.

Silently, Todd has left the camera and sat beside you on the sofa.

"What about the video," you murmur.

"It's running," he says. He wraps a long arm around your shoulders. For a minute you sit quietly together like this, watching the couple on the other sofa.

Jones is kissing her deeply, bending her head back. He has one hand between her thighs. You feel a quick pang of pain as you see her part her legs. Jones cups her mound through the red silk of her panties, and she quivers. You take a deep breath and lean into Todd.

XV

Todd is sitting calmly, sipping his rye and Coke, watching his wife and your boyfriend, is not looking at you. He lets his hand dangle over your breast as Jones did, brushing his palm against your nipple, making it hard. He smells of a soapy cologne.

He turns your shoulders slightly so your back leans against his chest, and strokes your arms with both his hands. You do not turn up to him, your eyes fixed on Jones and Anita, but you go limp, allow his hands to roam over you. You are going to let him touch you, you think, wherever he wishes. You try to relax as he cups your breasts, rubs circles on your bare belly. When his fingers delve into the waistband of your panties you push his hand away. You sit and watch Jones and Anita.

Jones is kneeling on the floor in front of her. His head is between her legs. He is kissing her crotch through her panties, blowing hot breath through the silk. You know how this feels, when Jones does it to you, and you watch now with a curious detachment.

She arches her neck back and moans. He slips his hands under her buttocks, liffting her up to his face. You squirm, thinking of how damp her panties must be becoming under his mouth.

You can feel Todd's cock stiffening against your back. It feels large. He is rubbing the cups of your bra with open palms now. It is not an unpleasant sensation. You relax a little against him, holding his knees with your hands. He is breathing deeply, moving his hips almost imperceptibly up and down so his cock rubs against your back. It grows larger and larger.

Jones is still on his knees, pulling Anita's panties off. She kicks them with one red pump so that they sail across the white carpet. She unclasps her bra and throws it after them, revealing large and sagging breasts with long nipples. They sway. Jones is snuffling in her crotch now, licking and sucking, his hands cupping her buttocks. Her back is arched now, and her moans are higher and sharper, becoming little yelps. Her nipples are stiff tubes; a mother's nipples. Her neck is flushed. Every now and then she opens her eyes a little to glance over at you and Todd, or maybe at the video camera, which is still whirring away, fixed on her.

Todd unclasps your bra; you let him. Your breasts fall out into the cool basement air. Todd clasps them gently with his meaty hands. You sigh. He runs his hands down your belly, keeps trying to get them inside your panties, and you keep pushing them away, although with less insistence.

Jones lifts himself up to lie on top of Anita, and she rolls out from under him. "Wait," she gasps. "Sit here."

She makes Jones sit while she opens a drawer in a side table and pulls out a roll of condoms. Now she kneels at Jones's feet, her back to you, and takes the purple head of his stiff cock into her mouth. She slides her mouth up and down the shaft, while sticking her ass up in the air. She parts her knees on the carpet, so that you can see the worn soles of her high-heeled shoes, her quivering thighs, her dimpled buttocks, the shiny crack between them where Jones has been licking. She looks raw and open.

Todd is stroking your crotch through your sheer panties, and it is making you pant. You make a decision: sit up, push his hand away. You can't concentrate on what his wife is doing to your boyfriend if you're too aroused. And you want to concentrate. You turn to Todd and undo his belt. Roughly, you unzip his fly and pull out his cock. It is thick, uncircumcised. The head is a shiny purple helmet, blunt and angry.

Todd stiffens, but does not moan or sigh. He is still watching his wife, her parted buttocks, her mouth stretched around Jones's cock.

You shift so you are sitting beside Todd. You tug his trousers and shorts down so they are around his ankles. You sit next to him and casually close your fingers around his stiff cock. Gently, slowly, you begin to stroke, up and down.

He pulls off his shirt. His chest and belly are hairy and strong.

Anita releases Jones's cock with an audible *plop*, and tears open the condom package. She rolls it over his cock. Then she stands to face you, tall and majestic in all her inflamed nakedness, her lipstick vanished, her face red, her nipples grotesquely long, her pubic hair trimmed and wet, her crotch slick, her mottled skin as naked as any skin you have ever seen. She smiles a confident smile and then, without turning around, lowers herself backwards onto Jones's cock. She leans forward, her eyes closed, as she reaches behind her to guide it in.

You watch Jones's long red cock, in its shiny plastic wrapping, disappear into her folds. She sits on him, facing you, her feet on the floor, her hands on her knees. Jones reaches around and holds her breasts in his hands. She begins to bob, to rise and fall, grinding herself down hard onto his cock so he groans, then slowly lifting herself up and staring down at it, between her legs, as it emerges, almost entirely, and just as the head is about to pop free she slams herself down again, gritting her teeth and closing her eyes.

You are jerking Todd's cock firmly now, and his breathing is hard. You feel it throb as you pull it up and down, squeezing ever tighter. He drops a hand to between your thighs and you let it stay there, clutching the inside of your thigh. Your eyes are fixed on Anita's body, her cunt stretched open and penetrated, her breasts flopping up and down as she bounces, her belly shaking, her head tossing back and forth, her gasps and grunts. All you can see of Jones is his legs, his hands grabbing at her waist and her breasts. His head is hidden behind her back. He drops one hand to her crotch, and begins circling her clit with his fingertip.

Anita begins to moan deeper and lower now. She leans forward, her hands on her knees, closes her eyes with concentration. Jones's hand is massaging, lightly, delicately, in circles. She begins to puff and pant. You can even see the shiny pink button of her clit emerging from its hood, pink and slick and hard, as Jones's fingertips flick at it, knead it.

Todd is puffing and panting too now, as he watches this as you pull on his cock, his hips jerking up and down, his mouth open.

You are excited too, but want to ignore it; you want to focus on Anita's climax, which approaches and recedes and approaches again: she stops jerking up and down for a second, starts to shudder and grimace, as Jones's fingers buzz over her clit, and then breathes deeply and begins fucking him again. Jones is plunging into her, from underneath her, as hard as he can, by pushing off his arched feet. He is grunting too, probably trying hard not to come inside her.

You rub your thighs together, jerk Todd as hard as you can. You wonder what Jones is seeing, from behind Anita, whether he is staring at her jiggling buttocks, his cock ramming in and out of her parted lips, her little asshole.

She has her eyes tight shut now, her jaws clenched. "Oh," she is hissing, in short bursts, through her teeth. "Oh. Oh. Oh." She throws her

111

head back and her orgasm begins: she shudders, hunches her shoulders, her jaw sinks to her chest as if she is concentrating, and then her body arches, her legs flail. She shrieks.

You are watching this with such absorption you are startled when Todd's cock spasms and bursts in your hand, throwing a cascade of heat over your fingers, your wrist, your forearm. You squeal, drawing back your hand as if scalded by the hot liquid, but Todd grabs your wrist, firmly holding your hand to his twitching cock, making you hold it for its final spurts. You squeeze the last drops from it as he breathes hard, wheezes, lets his head sink back, his mouth open. "Oh God," he whispers, letting go of your hand. You stroke his hair, lean against him as comfortingly as you can, while wiping the sticky white stuff on the sofa. (Where else can you wipe it? You don't want any of it on you, and you are practically naked.) You don't take your eyes off Anita, though, as she sinks back against Jones, kissing him wetly, writhing against him. She slides off his cock, revealing it to be, astoundingly, still hard, swaying as if angry to be abandoned.

She goes back down on her knees, on the floor, and carefully pulls the condom off it. She puts the shiny knob back into her mouth, encircles the base with her red-nailed fingers, and begins to suck and jerk him, fast and serious. You wonder if she minds the rubbery taste of condom.

Jones puts his fists on the sofa, lifts his ass off it a little so he can pump his hips, in and out of Anita's mouth. His face is red and tight; you can tell he wants to come. He is fucking Anita's mouth fast and hard. She restrains his plunging cock with her hand tight around its base. Her thumb is wet too, pressing firmly on the tender spot on the underside of the head, as it shuttles in and out of her mouth, stroking insistently.

Now you want to come. You pull off your underpants, then snuggle against Todd, sitting between his legs with your back against his hairy chest. You pull his hand into your crotch. You spread your legs as his fingers delve into you. You let them probe you for a minute, then you guide his hand to your clit, take two of his fingers and rub them over your sensitive little knot, in circles, lightly.

Obediently, he begins to stroke. He nuzzles your ear and cheek with his bristly moustache. You reach up and stroke his face, to be nice. But your eyes are still on Jones, his cock so deep in Anita's mouth, her cheek distended with the size of it, his stomach and chest clenched so tight, his face so desperate to come. You wonder if she really will let him come in her mouth, and wonder if you have ever let him do that. You don't think so.

You breathe deeply as you feel the buzzing in your clit begin, the warmth that is almost like a pain that spreads through your abdomen. Todd's fingers are gentle but fast, stroking, stroking. With the other hand he cups your breast, teases the nipple. You begin to pump your pelvis up and down in rhythm with his strokes. You feel hot, engulfed in Todd's strong flesh. His legs grip your legs, his hands hold you firm. You writhe, pinned by his fingers.

Jones is saying, "Oooh, oooh," his voice falling, as if surprised by a present he is opening. "Oooh! Oooh!"

Suddenly Anita jerks her head away, letting Jones's cock pop out, and it shoots a stream of white right over her shoulder. Jones yells as his cock pumps white semen into the air, onto her shoulder, onto her breast. She holds it at arm's length, jerking it with her hand, keeping her face well back from the spray and laughing.

Everybody laughs as Jones falls backwards, panting, everybody but you, because the sight of his cock spurting seed into the air was like a flame that pierced between your legs, firing your orgasm deep into your belly, out through your arms and legs. "Oh God," you wail, as you shudder against Todd, snapping your legs shut to trap his hand against your burning clit, to keep the waves coming. You close your eyes and let it flatten you like an ocean. Your muscles clench and release, clench and release, deep and fast. The tingling passes over them like sleep.

You are quiet for a while, leaning against Todd with your eyes closed. Everyone is quiet, lying still. The video camera hums.

You open your eyes and notice that everyone looks a little different. Anita is blinking her eyes, looking lined and old. Jones moves away from her on the sofa. He looks exhausted, and thin and awkward. His cock looks red and sore and shrunken.

You disengage from Todd, who is still pawing at your breast, and begin to look around for your clothes.

With a decisive click, the video camera stops. The tape has ended. Everyone laughs at this. Then Anita and Jones yawn simultaneously, which makes you all laugh again, and then everyone is looking for clothes.

In the taxi, you don't speak. Jones leans his head on your shoulder like a small child who needs to sleep. You hold his hand and stroke his neck and look out the window at the vast flying overpasses, amazed by how much traffic there is in this nowhere in the middle of the night.

XVI

Jones has a rental crisis. His roommate has moved out, to do a post-doc at some small American university whose name apparently means quite a lot to Jones but which you don't recognize (the fact that he assumes that you would recognize it means that you should recognize it, if you were educated, as you should be – all this makes you want to get a drastic haircut), and Jones can't afford the rent on his own. But it pains you both to imagine him giving up the flat in the Victorian brick house in the leafy blocks near the university, the flat with the high ceilings and the mouldings and the fireplace (which doesn't work, of course, but is symbolic of something, perhaps of being one step closer to a real fireplace), and the streets around with their overturned tricycles and their rotting apples and their academic women raking up leaves with their hair in wispy ponytails. It is a lovely apartment.

And you have never really been happy with your white box, with its small windows and its fire escape which the landlord called a deck. (Jones's apartment has a little roofed balcony off a turret, where pigeons nest, with an ornate wooden balustrade. The balcony is large enough for two cracked wooden chairs and a cafe table and a wine bottle with a candle stuck in it, at which you can sit at night and look down, drunk, on the passing bicycles.)

There are problems, of course, with Jones's apartment: the brown mouldings, painted in gloss oil by some previous tenant, the smell of laundry hamper, the tacked-up posters (for *Reservoir Dogs* and *Pulp Fiction*, for a Keith Haring exhibition of the mid-80s, for a Beck concert three years ago), the absence of lamps, the absence of wine glasses, indeed the absence of anything one might soberly call furniture. All these things can be corrected, by you of course – but it is the realization that none of them bothers Jones that truly depresses you, the knowledge that it has never occurred to him that one could paint over the brown paint left by a previous tenant, the knowledge that he is not aware that you might find his apartment mildly unattractive, not to say deeply, troublingly adolescent, this is what depresses you. You can fix his apartment, but can you fix Jones?

And then there is the general and unadmittable problem that you don't quite want to give up your own apartment, ugly and expensive as it is, that you don't know about giving up your nights alone at the bar at the Bar Verona or at the Meridien, eating rare steak and drinking red wine and meeting strange men in suits who tie you up and shave your pubic hair – this is something you probably shouldn't discuss with Jones. You could take him to the fetish club, you could take him to the suburban swing club, but the thing is . . . you did those things together. As a couple. Those things are less risky as a couple. Couples who do that are playing, playing mostly with each other: they know that each is watching over the other; they know that they are going to go home together.

But Jones doesn't know what you want to do alone. What you have done alone. You don't know how he could handle your taste for that dim, scented house in Yorkville, where Patrice and the shaved woman waited for you. A house of velvet and steel surfaces.

For a second you think of Patrice, as you often do, the phone call when you were in Vancouver. How he did not hesitate to try to get you to masturbate while you waited in an office, in front of the secretary. How he jerked off, whispering your name, on the other end of the telephone. His throaty cries.

But you hardly think of Patrice any more, you really don't. You have to think about this Jones question. And it is, in fact, your memories of your nights meeting strangers – for that is what Patrice is, after all, and always will be, a stranger – the fear that draws you to people who aren't like Jones at all, that decides you. It is time to stop the random sex with strangers. (Which Jones would gladly do; it makes you feel all warm for a second to realize that Jones wants only you.)

Anything could have happened in that suburban rec room with Todd and Anita, for example, in that muffled basement, so far from civilization. They could have put you in their freezer in neatly labelled Tupperwares.

You wonder at yourself. You wonder what thrill you will seek next.

You think you had better move in with Jones, accept his adolescent love. You will be safe with him. Before you get yourself killed.

Jones is delighted, of course, and so you begin the agony of packing up your apartment, of sorting through old books and trying to remember whom you lent what to, and the nostalgia of sorting through old letters, how you can spend the afternoon sitting on your bedroom floor surrounded by a pile of papers, reading and laughing and crying. You put this off as long as you can. You wrap up your paintings, the little prints by friends. You put off thinking about how you are going to move the jagged gear-wheel sculpture that cinematographer made for you.

Soon your apartment is awash in rolling dustballs. The emptier it gets, the lonelier you get. You have a first-day-of-school pit in your belly.

You know it will pass once you set up house with Jones. You distract yourself by what colours you will paint his living room, what tiles you will install in the mouldy bathroom.

Jones says he will take you out to dinner every night on the last week before your move, so you don't have to face your empty apartment, which makes you feel so touched you could cry. In fact you do cry. You are a little edgy this week.

You are preparing for the first of these dinners – rummaging through a lingerie drawer; the lingerie will be the last thing you pack up – when there is a ring at the door.

You answer in your dressing gown.

There is a courier bearing a bunch of huge white flowers. They are orchids. They come with a letter. Your name on the envelope is not in Jones's handwriting.

As slowly as you can, you take the flowers into the kitchen and put them down. You force yourself to find a vase and put them in water before you open the letter. Your hands are trembling as you cut the ends off the stems.

You take the letter into your bare bedroom, and sit on the bed in a square of afternoon sun. You sit on the rumpled bed and hold the letter. Your heart is thumping.

You tear open the letter.

You read the first line and a quiver goes through your body that makes you want to be naked, be naked or flee, fold up the letter and throw it away.

The first line reads:

Diana,
This is what I am going to do to you.

117

You sigh, close your eyes. You know you should not read the rest of this letter. You pull open your dressing gown and put your hand to your crotch. Your sex has suddenly grown moist. You know you will read the rest of the letter.

As you read, you stretch out on the bed, spread your legs. You dip your fingers into your sex. You want something inside you, something to fuck you and fill you.

The letter says this:

Diana,

This is what I am going to do to you. I am going to invite a group of people to my studio to watch you. The people will be old and rich and young and beautiful, men and women. I will dress you in a white gauze dress that blows in the wind and shows your nipples as smudges, your pubic hair as a shadow. When I stand you in front of the window your form is silhouetted in the light, the dress blowing around you like mist. I will stand you on a dais and they will crowd around to watch me as I caress you, as I lift your white gauze dress over your head and lay you on the divan on the dais. I will pull the cloth off you so your breasts and your belly and your little tuft of hair are exposed to the visitors. I will lift your arms over your head and spread your legs, so you are helpless, and I will ask the people one by one to approach you, admire you, touch you. You cannot move. In the cool breeze from the window your nipples stiffen, the strangers' hands pass over your body, softly, stroking and grasping. They rub your breasts, they pass their fingers up the inside of your thighs. I stand at your head, stroking your temples and watching. When one woman attempts to kiss your furry mound, I wave her away. They stand to one side, excited, jostling together, to watch as I strip off my clothes, stand between your legs with my cock proud. I take your nipples in my mouth, one by one, bending over you, and you can feel the head of my cock brushing against your entrance, your furry lips. You tense and wait for me to push it in. But I don't push it in; I run my mouth down your belly, slowly, towards your cleft, I gently lick at your lips, parting them with my tongue, wetting them, darting my tongue in and out, then flicking at your stiffening little clit, circling it with my tongue, so you are writhing and quivering on the divan,

118

in front of all those people, watching the veins in your neck, your jig-gling breasts, your tender underarms with their exposed stubble, all naked and all those people seeing all of you, every secret inch of you, as you become excited and embarrassed that you are excited – and that's when I will ram my cock into you, plunge it deep and pull your legs up to around my shoulders and fuck you hard, so that your ass jiggles and my balls slap against it, so that you grit your teeth and clutch your thighs, holding them up in the air so I can slam into you deeper, and then I will lie on top of you, slowing down and holding my cock still, so I can grind my pubes against yours, rubbing your clit with my body until you start to gasp and shudder, and then I will pull out, suddenly, before you come. And then I will stand back and select a man from the crowd, a young man, an anonymous man, and I will strip off his trousers so that his cock springs free, already erect and enlarged, and I will stand back so that he can ram his cock into you, sweat and grunt over you, staring at your face, at your averted eyes. And despite yourself you feel yourself coming close to orgasm again. You try to restrain your cries. But I reach between your belly and his, I reach down into your groin and find your little button, as he slams into you with his swollen cock, and I caress it, gently, in cir-cles, until you cannot restrain yoursef any more, you burst, biting hard on your lip so as not to make too much noise, you thrash and jerk your pelvis against his, your eyes closed, fucking this stranger as much as he is fucking you, spitting and swearing, "Yes, yes, oh fuck, fuck you, fuck, yes, fuck me, please, fuck, oh fuck." You feel other hands on your shoulders, pinning you down so you cannot thrash too much. And when you are still shivering and quivering, I pull him off you so that I can have the final pleasure, I lie with my whole weight on you and thrust my cock into your slick hole, and I come right away, splashing my sperm into you and pushing, pushing as hard as I can. I pull away and you are dripping, your thighs wet and shiny, you are beautiful and tender. The crowd is breathing hard with lust for you.

This is how I think of you, my love, all the time; you are my obses-sion, my lust. I am filled with desire for you wherever I am. I lust for you everywhere. I want always to fuck you deeply, fuck you every-where, fuck your cunt, fuck your mouth, penetrate you, fill you, come on you, come all over you, spill my semen all over you, spurt it on

119

your pristine white skin, come on your breasts, on your tight little belly, on your round buttocks, I want to come in your mouth and see it spilling out onto your chin, overflowing, I want to spurt in your asshole and see it dripping out between your thighs, I want to see you come and moan and writhe, I want to see you come and come, I want you to fuck me, jerk me, suck me, dominate me, penetrate me, then I want to kiss your trembling skin, your lips, your belly, your cunt lips dripping with sperm, I want to lick you and suck you and hold your tongue with mine, while my cock throbs inside you, I want to love you, my wet skin stuck to yours. I will love you like no other.

Meet me at 9 o'clock tonight at my studio. I must see you. I only have tonight; I go away again at midnight.
Patrice

You sit for a long time in the long afternoon sun, watching the light angle lower, growing warmer, yellower, on your bare skin spread out on the bed. Your apartment is very quiet. Your crotch is burning, throbbing, but you do not touch it. It is too dangerous.

Finally you rise and go to the telephone. You call Jones. You say, "Hi," and pause.

He says, "Hi. Are we still on for tonight?" There is old funky music in the background. *Shaka Khan, Shaka Khan Khan.* For some reason it makes him seem vulnerable. You feel sad to hear it.

"Well, that's the thing. Something's come up." You hesitate again, feeling very far away from Jones. You don't know yet what you are going to tell him. But you are going to tell him something. You are going to make something up. "Listen. Is it okay if I cancel tonight?"

"Sure. What's wrong?"

"Nothing. Nothing. It's just that . . . I'm kind of on a roll with the packing, and I think I can get a lot done tonight. I can't believe how behind I am."

"Sure. But you can go back to it after we eat."

"I'm not hungry anyway."

"Diana, you have to eat. What's the matter? Is something wrong?"

"No, no, nothing. But Denise called, too, and she wants to see me before I move. I haven't seen her in so long. So I thought I'd go out for a drink with her. You know, just girls kind of thing."

120

"I thought you had to pack."

You feel like crying for Jones. But you can't stop it. You are going to see Patrice tonight, one last time. And then never again. "Yeah, I'm going to pack for a while, and then I'll go out for a drink with her at around ten. A quick one."

Jones is silent for a moment. "Do you want me to meet you afterwards?"

"No, that's okay. I think . . . I think I need to sleep alone tonight. Before we sleep together every night, you know what I mean?" You give a quick giggle.

Jones laughs. "Okay, baby. I get it. Enjoy your last gasp of freedom."

"You don't mind?"

"Of course I don't mind. I understand. Say hi to Denise for me."

When you hang up your belly burns from guilt. The pain you feel for Jones is clear and fine and cold, like pure alcohol. You shake your head to dispel it. Jones will never know. This is the last time.

You take your time dressing. You choose a gauzy dress, like the one you first wore to visit Patrice in his studio that rainy spring. You wear your blue lacy bra, white cotton panties, and bare legs.

121

XVII

You arrive early; the sun has not yet set. The warehouse building looks unchanged. A light rain has begun. You step out of the taxi and shiver. The streets in this industrial district are empty, grey. You feel a little nervous as you step towards the loading docks, the fire escapes of this squat brick block. Heavy clouds move with determination overhead. You walk up the wide factory stairwells. They smell of fresh paint.

The big double doors to Patrice's studio are wide open. You stand in the doorway for a moment, watching him, before he sees you. He has a big black duffel bag open on the coffee table, and he is throwing clothes into it. His studio seems empty; there are cardboard boxes everywhere. There are no framed prints on the walls. The stereo is disconnected. Patrice is humming to himself. His hair is shorter, spiky and dishevelled. He has his usual blond stubble on his face, and is wearing his usual tight undershirt and worn leather jeans. He is deeply tanned, and wears some kind of ethnic bracelets on his wrists: silver bangles rattle on his left, beaded ones on his right. He is still strong and fit, but looks tougher somehow, wirier, as if he has been living rough.

You stand still in the doorway until he sees you. Then he stops, smiles, and stretches his arms towards you. You both run at each other and collide. You kiss and laugh and kiss; you clasp his strong arms, rub your face like a cat over his stubbly chin. He touches you all over, stroking your bare arms, your back, your buttocks. He touches your breasts, and you let your head fall back, limp and pliant, for him to kiss your neck. You grab his buttocks, rub your hips against his. You want him to rip your dress off and push you back onto the sofa.

But he doesn't: he pulls away, takes you by the hand to the sofa, where he sits you down. He goes to the fridge, pulls out a cold bottle of white wine. You cross your legs. Your body feels like a humming electrical wire. Your dress feels like a blanket on a hot night; you want to toss it off, writhe naked before him.

He puts the bottle in a silver ice bucket on the table. He puts two wine glasses beside it, and sits with you. But he does not push the big black

122

duffel bag out of the way. You stare at it, at the clothes stacked inside. He has filled it with khaki shirts with big pockets.

"Where are you travelling?" you say.

He is pouring the wine. "This is the same wine," he says, "that you had when you first came here."

"I noticed."

He leans back into the sofa and looks at you, narrowing his eyes as he appraises you, up and down. He passes his eyes over your bare legs, stares at your chest. You turn towards him to accommodate his gaze. You hike your dress up a little on your thighs, stretch them out before him. Then you push the straps of your dress off your shoulders. You shake your hair loose. You open your mouth slightly and look him in the eyes. You want him to take you here and now, on this cool leather sofa. You don't have much time; you want to be home before midnight.

"Cheers," he says.

"Cheers." The wine is icy, lemons and honey. You look at his wiry frame, his tanned arms, and want him.

He stands, puts his wine down, and walks across the room to a chest of drawers. He begins pulling out linen shirts, a vest full of pockets, some kind of map case, tubes of sunscreen. He throws them into the duffel bag.

"Are you going away for long?"

"I'm going away for good."

"For good." The words are cold in your mouth. There is a weight in your belly. "Why . . . why would you do that?"

He shrugs. "I have to." He goes into the bathroom, emerges with bottles of pills and lotions, throws them into the bag.

"What about to your house in Yorkville? Are you packing that up, too?"

"I told you it wasn't my house."

"Whatever."

He looks at you and smiles. "Yes, it was my house. I gave it away."

"You *gave* it away."

He shrugs.

"You must have a lot of money to do that."

He pulls the mosquito netting down from around the bed, folds it neatly and throws it into the bag.

But it's not the house you want to talk about. Trying to laugh, you say, "What about me?"

"You're welcome to come with me."

"Sure."

"I mean it," he says quietly.

You are silent for a moment, sipping your wine. "I'm about to move in with my boyfriend."

He doesn't reply.

You say, "I'm all packed up and ready to move. Next week."

Patrice begins to whistle as he packs.

"Are you listening to me?" You stand, walk over to him. "I'm moving in with a guy. For good." You wrap your arms around him, rub your face in his neck, smelling him. "This is our last chance."

"No it's not. You're coming with me."

"Come on. Don't be silly." You grind your hips against his thighs, feeling his cock swell against your belly. A hard leather lump. You grab his hand, put it under your skirt, on your ass. He kisses you deeply, his tongue moving in your mouth. You are trembling, trying to wrap your legs around him without falling over. He moves his hand to your crotch, cups your mound through the white cotton panties.

"Oooh," you say. "Oh." You stand still as he strokes you there, gently, through the cotton, your legs shaking. "Oh God," you whisper. "Take them off. Take me. Take me now. Please."

"No," he murmurs. He strokes you through the panties. You can feel your wetness seeping out. "Oh God. Oh fuck." You cling to him tightly, hanging from his neck. You are breathing hard. "Oh. I'm going to come. I'm going to come just standing here." You grab his belt buckle, fumble with it. You want his cock inside you.

Quickly, he pulls away. "No time," he says. "I've got to go." He zippers up his duffel bag, leaving you standing there, panting, your crotch aching. You feel dizzy.

"You bastard."

He picks up the phone.

"What are you doing?"

"Can I have a cab at forty-five Ellis please?"

"Patrice, wait." You lift your skirt, pull your panties off.

"The entry code is oh four three."

124

You throw your panties at him. He brushes them off.

"To the airport. Thank you."

"Make love to me."

Patrice hangs up. "I will make love to you for the rest of your life if you come with me."

"Will you stop with that. Don't be ridiculous."

He sits on the sofa, pours you some more wine.

You fall on him, straddle him, rub your naked crotch against his leather. "Please."

He kisses your neck and chest, tenderly. "I'm the one who should be saying please. Please come with me."

"Patrice, I'm not going to give up my whole life. I don't even know where you're going."

"Does it matter?"

You are silent for a long moment.

He pulls the straps of your dress down farther. You wriggle your arms free. He pulls your dress to your waist. Your breasts fall free. He kisses your nipples. They harden.

He says, kissing your breasts, "I will take care of you. You have to trust me. That's why you don't even need to know where we're going."

"I don't have any clothes with me. I couldn't even go anywhere for a short time. Oh God that feels good."

"We'll buy you clothes when we get there. Besides, you don't need many clothes where we're going."

"I don't have any money."

"I do. More than enough."

"Patrice." You reach for his belt buckle again. He lets you undo it, unbutton his jeans. You grab the knob of his hard cock, pull it out from his shorts. It is shiny and full, pretty as a flower. He flinches a little, but does not move. You want to take it in your mouth, make it wet. You slide down, begin stroking it with both hands. You kiss it gently, just as a bubble of clear liquid is forming at its tip. You taste its salt.

"I have to go. My taxi."

"Make love to me once before you go."

"No. You have to come with me." He throws you off, jumps to his feet, pulling up his trousers. You fall to the floor, your dress loose and falling around your thighs.

"You bastard." You get up, pull your dress back up. "Why did you even ask me here?" You find your panties on the floor and put them on. You feel hot and angry. And the idea of Patrice leaving forever is like a clear, burning pain in your blood. You think, suddenly, that you will cry. You know you are being crazy, that it will pass. You try to think of Jones, but can hardly even picture him.

"To ask you to come with me. That's why I asked you here. Because I love you."

"No, you don't."

"Trust me." He gets up, begins switching off lights. He checks the stove. "Drink your wine," he says.

"I can't. I feel sick." Your heart is pounding crazily.

He throws some sheets over the remaining furniture.

"I'm in love with someone else," you say.

"No you're not."

You try to laugh again. "How do *you* know I'm not?"

"I know you," he says calmly.

You grab your glass of wine from the coffee table. You gulp from it. "No, I'm not."

There is a faint honking from outside.

"There's my cab."

"That was fast," you say. "That was way too fast to be your cab. It can't be yours."

He is lifting the huge duffel bag off the table, swinging it onto his shoulder. "Let's go."

He walks to the door. You follow him into the wide, empty, paint-smelling hallway. You feel sick. Your throat is choked up. He locks the big swinging doors with a padlock.

The cab honks again. Through the wide factory window in the stair-well you can see the car below, waiting in the empty parking lot, a red and yellow car on black concrete. It is still raining. The asphalt is slick. You can almost hear the echoing announcements in the airport, feel the excite-ment of the blinking monitors, the signs listing gate numbers. "Red and yellow are the colours of death," you say.

He laughs, begins walking down the stairs. You follow him. "No," he says. "The colours of life. Of adventure."

In the parking lot you stop. You watch him walk across the asphalt to

126

the taxi. The taxi driver leans across and opens the passenger door. It swings wide open. The interior of the taxi is dark, leathery.

"Well, goodbye," you call. "At least say goodbye to me."

He says nothing, opens the trunk of the car and swings his bag inside. He gets in the back seat and slides across, away from you. He leaves the door open.

"Come on," he calls. "We'll get you a toothbrush at the airport."

The rain has begun to fall more heavily. You stand on the black asphalt, getting wet. Your thin dress clings to your breasts. The taxi has the owner's name painted on the door: *T. Tod.* The taxi driver stares at you: he is white, so white he looks colourless, like a ghost. He is wearing some kind of silly hat: a boatman's cap with a visor. You cannot believe you are noticing these details right now. Everything seems very clear. The driver stares at you impassively, as if he knows that you are coming too. He glances back at Jones. Then he looks straight ahead, waiting.

"Is it a long flight?" you call.

"Very."

"Then I'll . . . I'll need a sweater."

He laughs from inside the cab. "Why?"

"Those planes are too air-conditioned. I'll get cold."

"Okay. We'll get you a sweater."

You stand still in the rain, getting cold. Your heart is pounding so hard and fast it is almost painful. You look at the cab, the open door. The inside of the cab is so black you can't make out the seats. It's a door to darkness. But you know somehow it would be warmer inside it. The warmth would have something to do with not making any more decisions.

You look at the cab driver's inhuman face; he is staring straight ahead. You turn and look at the huge old warehouse building, blackening with rain. The streets around are deserted. You don't remember how to get home from here. There is a thunderclap.

"Come on," calls Patrice. "You'll freeze."

"No. Goodbye."

Patrice says nothing. The car does not move.

You take a deep breath, and run, blindly, towards the waiting taxi, the black space, the flames, the open door.

THE END

Russell Smith is the author of six works of fiction. A well-known journalist and cultural commentator, he writes a weekly column on language and culture in *The Globe and Mail*.

His first novel, *How Insensitive*, was nominated for the Governor General's Award, the Trillium Award, and became a best-seller. He is also the author of the novels *Noise* and *Muriella Pent*, the short story collection *Young Men*, the illustrated fable *The Princess and the Whiskheads*, and a book on men's fashion, *Men's Style*. He lives and writes in Toronto.